Rollo in Emblemland

Rollo
in Emblemland

A tale inspired by
Lewis Carroll's Wonderland

by John Kendrick Bangs and
Charles Raymond Macauley

ILLUSTRATIONS BY
CHARLES RAYMOND MACAULEY

evertype

2010

Published by Evertype, Cnoc Sceichín, Leac an Anfa, Cathair na Mart, Co. Mhaigh Eo, Éire. *www.evertype.com*.

First edition New York: R. H. Russell, 1902.
Original title: *Emblemland*.

A catalogue record for this book is available from the British Library.

ISBN-10 1-904808-58-1
ISBN-13 978-1-904808-58-9

Typeset in De Vinne Text, Mona Lisa, ENGRAVERS' ROMAN, and *Liberty* by Michael Everson.

Edited by Michael Everson.

Illustrations: Charles Raymond Macauley, 1902.

Cover: Michael Everson.

Printed by LightningSource.

Foreword

*J*ohn Kendrick Bangs (1862–1922) was born in Yonkers, New York, and is known for his work as an author, editor, and satirist. In 1884 he became an Associate Editor of *Life*, later working at *Harper's Magazine, Harper's Bazaar,* and *Harper's Young People*, in the position of "Editor of the Departments of Humor" for all three from 1889 to 1900. Later he worked as editor of *Munsey's Magazine*, of Harper's *Literature*, and of the *New Metropolitan* magazine, and in 1904 he was appointed editor of *Puck*, perhaps the foremost American humour magazine of its day.

Bangs made two contributions to the Carrollian world. *Emblemland* was the first, written in 1902 together with Charles Macauley. Caroline Sigler calls this "an *Alice*-like fantasy", in which a young American boy named Rollo visits a strange country peopled with symbols and icons. Macauley's line drawings are charming and some of the verse in the book is reminiscent of Carroll's.

Bangs' second contribution was made in 1907. In *Alice in Blunderland: An Iridescent Dream*, Bangs makes light of a range of economic issues as familiar to his contemporary readers as they are to us today: high taxes, corporate greed, bribery, institutional corruption, and governmental incompetence are among its themes.

The signature on page 2 is Bangs', scanned in from a copy of *Alice in Blunderland* book which I acquired last year. The photograph here is of Bangs in 1922, shortly before his death.

Although the language Bangs uses is quite American, he made use of a number of British spellings, such as "practised" and "centre". Accordingly I have regularized the text to conform to Oxford orthography, though some dialect spellings have been given their more standard forms, as "how-di-doo" has been changed to "how-d'ye-do". I preferred adjectival "moonlit" to "moonlight" in one place. The Irish dialect spelling of Santa Claus' carpenter Jimmie has been tweaked so that it better reflects the intended pronunciation.

Other spellings have been normalized: "wabbly" to "wobbly", "hi!" to "hey!", "hoh!" to "ho!", "good-by" to "good-bye", "scare-cat" to "scaredy-cat", "hullo" to "hello", "bowlder" to "boulder". For style, "8,000,000" has been spelled out "eight million".

Now, ordinarily, I am not much of a fan of overzealous political correctness, but 1902 was a different time, and a few elements in Bangs' story rather get in the way of reading pleasure today. None of these are essential to the story, but for completeness sake, I'll note that the verb "ejaculated" has been changed to "exclaimed" and the verb "fags" to "tires"; the epithet "niggeramus" has been restored to "ignoramus", and the line "Piccaninnies for the black" has been changed to "Sleepy babies hit the sack". Bangs isn't really to be blamed for using these terms, but the story is easier to read without them. Similarly, Bangs occasionally had some of his characters say "ain't" for "isn't" and "'em" for "them". By and large, Bangs' use of these words these did not really add anything to characterization or mood; the standard form has been preferred, except in the Crocodile's poem on page 60, in the Sandman's poem on page 94, and throughout the Eagle's dialogue, since his use of "'em" seems quite natural.

In general, Bangs' punctuation has been altered to conform to modern practice. In places I have followed Carrollian practice: "to-day", and "to-night" are all hyphenated, for instance, and since Bangs had written "sha'n't", I have indulged in applying Carroll's preference for the spellings "ca'n't" and "wo'n't".

Though the book's original title was *Emblemland*, I have preferred the longer title *Rollo in Emblemland*, given by Bangs in the last sentence of the story.

Michael Everson
Westport, August 2010

Sigler, Carolyn. 1997. *Alternative Alices: Visions and revisions of Lewis Carroll's* Alice *books*. Lexington: University Press of Kentucky. ISBN 0-8131-2028-4

Sigler, Carolyn. 2008. "Alice Imitations" in *The Oxford Encyclopedia of Children's Literature*, vol. 1, pp 47–49. Oxford: Oxford University Press. ISBN 978-0-19-514656-1

Rollo in Emblemland

John Kendrick Bangs

Contents

Chapter I

Rollo Enters Emblemland

Somehow or other, although he could not account for it at all, it seemed to Rollo to be the most natural thing in the world. Of course, it was strange that he should be out there on the great, broad blue sea in a wobbly old boat, without a sail or an oar, with nobody but the Dolphin along to keep him company, but while it was all happening it did not strike Rollo as being half so extraordinary as a thousand and one other things he had seen at the country circus a week before. As he said to his brother Teddy afterward, "There I was in that awfully rocky boat, with no land in sight, and the Dolphin just sitting there and grinning all the time, and it didn't seem any more queerer than asking for a second piece of pie."

"Which is the most naturalest thing in the world," said Teddy, a young man of six with a wide experience in pies and other toothsome things.

"Oh, yes, indeed," Rollo answered. "More naturaler than getting it, most of the time," referring, of course, to the second piece of pie so often sought and so frequently denied.

Just how he got into such a strange craft, as well as into the still stranger company of the Dolphin, Rollo never was able quite to explain, and, as a matter of fact, he never tried very hard to do so. He knew from the beginning that some things were impossible of explanation, and was wise accordingly.

"I'd just come home from Neddy Tomlinson's advertisement party," he said when talking the matter over later with his father, "where I'd been having a bully time all the afternoon disguised all up as one of the Coal Dust Twins, and getting off jokes with boys from Soapless Town, and eating chicken salad and sponge-cake by the pound. You and Ma weren't home yet, so I sat down before the fire to think, when all of a sudden there I was, not before the fire at all, but sitting in the middle of the boat, whizzing over the sea, and the Dolphin looking at me with a squizzical look in his eye."

"Paid your fare?" asked the Dolphin, severely, after the boat had run on for a little.

"No," said Rollo, shortly. "Have you?"

"I didn't have to," retorted the Dolphin, with a complacent grin. "I get my ride free for my services as Captain, Mate, Bosun, Crew, Pilot, Cabin-boy, Stevedore too, which I beg to remind you is poetry. Too and crew—eh? Pretty good, *I* think. If you haven't paid your fare," he continued, "I'm afraid I'll have to put you off. Ca'n't travel on this line without a ticket, you know."

"Put me off?" cried Rollo, aghast, looking out over the sea and finding no sign of land in sight. "Out here in all this wet?"

It was dreadfully wet, as the ocean always is.

"Why not? Got your rubbers on, haven't you?" demanded the Dolphin.

"But it's over my head," pleaded Rollo.

"Ho!" jeered the Dolphin. "So is the sky. What of it?"

"But I ca'n't swim," protested Rollo. "You wo'n't put me off way out here, will you, and let me get drownded?"

"You might work your passage," said the Dolphin, reflecting a moment, and scratching his head with one of his fins as if to loosen up his ideas. "The only thing is, all the positions on this boat are already filled. There isn't a single vacancy."

"Couldn't I be a sailor before the mast?" asked Rollo.

"Not very well," said the Dolphin. "You see, there's two reasons why not. I'm all the sailors we have on board, and then, again, there isn't any mast for you to be a sailor before."

A happy thought flashed across Rollo's brain.

"Maybe I might be the mast," he said, eagerly. "I'm pretty strong and stiff."

"No, I don't think you could," said the Dolphin. "You— you're too short. You'd make a better bowsprit—then you're too fleshy and not woody enough, and I don't think you'd do before the fury of a gale. Did you ever see the fury of a gale?"

"No, I never did," Rollo confessed, for he never had.

"Well, it's perfectly awful. Most furiousest thing you ever saw," returned the Dolphin. "Ever work a bellows?" he added.

"Oh, yes—lots of times," said Rollo. "I've blown up the library-fire with our bellows heaps of times."

7

"Well, a gale isn't a bit like a bellows, so you see what a horrid time you would have holding up a sail before it. I tell you what might be done, though," the Dolphin continued. "The Cabin-boy might resign, and I could engage you to take his place."

"Where is he?" asked Rollo.

"I'm him," said the Dolphin. "Get me a piece of paper and a pen and some ink, and I'll write to myself as Captain, resigning as Cabin-boy."

"I haven't any pen and ink and paper with me," said Rollo, who had never thought of travelling about with such things just as if they were knives and marbles and pieces of string, or other similar necessities of life.

"Careless boy!" cried the Dolphin. "Brought no writing materials at all? Going to sea without even a pencil? My goodness!

> *"Going to travel across the sea*
> *Without no ink nor paper?*
> *It certainly appears to me*
> *A mighty careless caper!*
> *Suppose the boat should spring a leak*
> *Some place where storms had rot it*
> *And wet should come in like a streak,*
> *What WOULD you do to blot it?*
> *Suppose the boat turned upside down*
> *With no one here to sight it?*
> *I greatly fear you'd have to drown*
> *Without a pen to write it."*

"Well, I didn't expect to come anyhow," said Rollo, indignantly, as he thought of the position he was in and how little he had had to do with it. "I haven't even brought a clean collar along."

"Nor a pair of andirons, either, I fancy—careless boy!" retorted the Dolphin, sarcastically. "And see what kind of a fix it's got you into, not having a bottle of ink in your pocket! There being no ink to resign with, the Cabin-boy ca'n't resign, and so there's no place for you on board, and I've just simply merely got to put you off, wet or no wet. I hate to do it, especially in view of your not having a clean collar or a pair of andirons, but rules is rules, and rules No. 10, 39, 46, and 312 says distinctly—no free rides on these here boats."

Again Rollo had a happy thought. "Ca'n't you discharge the Cabin-boy for being imperant?"

"Being what?" queried the Dolphin, cocking his head to one side and gazing at Rollo in a mystified fashion.

"Imperant—sassy—muttinous—" Rollo began.

"Oh, *mutinous*, you mean," laughed the Dolphin as he realized what Rollo meant. "Well, that is a good idea. Me as Cabin-boy rebel against me as Captain—eh? That it?"

"That's it," said Rollo.

"It might be done," said the Dolphin, "for you see, my dear Rollo, I'm a very strict Captain and a very bad Cabin-boy, due to my pride in both capacities, and under such circumstances it isn't hard for a Cabin-boy to get saucy. Yes, I'll do it. Just wait a minute."

Rollo watched the singular creature with staring eyes, as he went through a most absurd performance.

"Hi there, you, Jimmie!" the Dolphin cried aloud as Captain, drawing himself up proudly.

"Yessir," he immediately replied as Cabin-boy, with a proper bow of respect—to himself.

"Brace the main halyards; let go the starboard sardines, and collect the eggs in the mizzen hatchways. Be quick about it, boy!" he roared, as Captain, puffing out his chest.

"That isn't my business. Captain Dolphin," he replied as Cabin-boy, and very angrily at that. "I'll polish the leescuppers and sweep out the garboard-strakes, but shiver my timbers if I'll do a cook's work, Captain Dolphin. Collect your own eggs."

"What?" cried the Captain. "This to me!"

"Yes, Captain Dolphin," he retorted as the boy. "That to you, and three times thrice as much more, sir, *an'* to your face!"

"Avast there!" the Captain roared. "Out upon you. Forth you go. *You're discharged*, an' lucky you are I put you not in irons. Overboard with you!"

And then something happened that Rollo had not reckoned upon. Overboard the Dolphin went, and his position would have been perilous indeed had it not also happened at the very same moment that the queer old row-boat struck upon a strange beach with such force that Rollo's legs flew up in the air and his head took up a position in the bottom of the boat which had hitherto been occupied by the planking of the vessel itself. Had this not been very thick and tough, I fear Rollo's head would have been buried in the sand underneath the keel.

He righted himself as quickly as he could and looked anxiously about for his companion, but there was no sign of him anywhere.

"Cap-tain Dol-phin!" Rollo hallooed through his hands after he had scrambled ashore. "Cap-tain Do–o–ol-phe–e–en!"

But there was no answer. The Dolphin apparently had other business in hand, or had felt himself so outraged by his severe treatment at the hands of his skipper that he proposed to have nothing more to do with the craft from which he had been discharged. It may be, too, that he feared the results of his mutiny, for it is a very serious thing for a member of a ship's company to defy the Captain on the high-seas as the Cabin-boy had done, and it is possible that he wished to hide himself from his prosecutors as speedily as he could in the mysterious depths of the wonderful ocean.

Now, Rollo was a boy who was not easily disturbed by the things that happened to him. He was a brave little chap, and had a way of making the best of everything. Since he was a baby he had not been known to cry over the unpleasant things that came into his life that he could not help; and so, suddenly cast away on a strange shore, instead of giving way to his fears as he might naturally have done, he was as comfortable in his mind as if he were safe at home. Hence it was that, having done all he could to call Captain Dolphin back, as much for company as for anything else, Rollo turned about and walked up the beach upon which he had been cast, resolved to investigate it and its contents as fully as his time would permit.

It was like all other beaches that Rollo had ever visited. Plenty of sand, no end of sea-weed, and beautiful shells without number—some of them were more beautiful than Rollo had ever seen before. But this time it was different in a single way. When Rollo had been a visitor at beaches before, it had always been in company with his father and mother. It is true, he had tried often to get away from them and to play by himself just to show how well he could take care of himself when left alone, but rarely had he been successful in escaping their watchful eye. If the truth were told, the best of Rollo's playmates, he thought, was his Papa, and Rollo many and many a time had said that he liked his daddy, old as he was— his daddy must have been at least thirty years of age—as a playmate even better than Neddy Tomlinson, who was one of the finest and sweetest boys in the world, even if he was occasionally too fond, Rollo thought, of having his own way. But his daddy had had a way of looking after Rollo's health when they went out playing together which Rollo deemed wholly unnecessary—it interfered so much with his fun. And now had come a glorious opportunity to disport himself on the shore of an unknown land, alone and self-reliant.

"Now that I am looking after myself," said Rollo, "I really wish I had my rubbers on. At any rate, I shall not sit down in the wet sand because—I really don't want to. It isn't any fun when there isn't anybody around to stop you."

The lad walked along, picked up many a rare shell, and then threw it down upon the sands again to pick up another that seemed still more rare and more beautiful. And then all of a sudden, realizing how truly alone he was, he began to feel a trifle uneasy. He was not frightened, for there was nothing here to frighten him; but he just didn't like it, it was so lonesome. His uneasiness did not last long, however, for hardly had he gone one hundred yards along the beach when he caught sight of a slender pole rising up out of the stretch of sand before him. From the top of it fluttered a piece of material that at a distance resembled a flag.

"Hello!" cried Rollo. "This isn't a desert island, after all. Somebody must have put that there. Let's see what it is."

And he ran toward it. It was the American flag that fluttered from the top of the slender pole, and, for the first time in his life, Rollo knew what the sight of those stars and of those stripes meant to one who is in a far, strange country. The comfort of the colours, the pride of its meaning, the spirit that it told of, all flashed over the boy's mind in a moment.

"Hurrah!" he cried, a great wave of happiness sweeping over him as he saw what the fluttering bunting was, and then he hurrahed again. "I've always been safe under that," said Rollo. "What next, I wonder?"

"What next?" came a voice from out of the forest that bordered the coast-line of this strange new country. "What next? Well, for me, give me a boost so that I may climb this tree."

Rollo looked about him and was much amused to see a pleasant-looking old gentleman, in a frock-coat and high silk-hat, two-thirds of the way up the trunk of a tall birch tree, struggling as hard as he could to reach the branches above him.

"Give me a boost, I tell you," cried the old gentle, fiercely, but smiling pleasantly withal, "I want to get up, and I'm losing my grip."

Rollo laughed. "What for?" he asked. "Why should a gentleman like you want to climb that tree?"

"Oh, merely to come down again, that's all," said old gentleman. "I've been told that the most successful men in the world have had their ups and downs, and, since I am very anxious to be successful, I'm taking that course. I'm doing the ups now. Hurry up and give me that boost, wo'n't you, or I shall be late with the downs!"

"I'd be glad to if I could," said Rollo, "but I ca'n't reach you. I'm too short."

"Get your step-ladder, then," cried the old gentleman, rather sharply.

"I haven't got one," said Rollo.

"Well, of all things!" cried the old gentleman. "Coming here without a step-ladder! Where *were* you brought up?"

Much as he liked the old gentleman's smile, Rollo was rather displeased by his manner. It wasn't *his* fault that the old gentleman was unable to climb the tree.

"I was brought *up* at home," said he. "But I've suddenly been brought *down* here without being asked whether I wanted to come or not. Why didn't you bring a step-ladder yourself?"

"Because," said the old gentleman, "my beaver hat is all I can carry on my mind at once. *Please* give me a boost."

"I'll do better," said Rollo. "I'll give you a lift," and in a moment he had shinned up the tree, and stood in its branches looking out over the country. Then, reaching out his hand, he grasped the old gentleman firmly by the collar, and working together they soon had him up where he wished to be.

"Where are we, Mister—?" Rollo began.

"I'm not a mister, I'm a *Judge*," said the old gentleman. "That's why I've climbed up here—just to get a lofty view of things."

"Very well. Judge," said Rollo. "Where are we? What country is this?"

"Well," said the Judge, "to answer that, I must reflect a little. Let—me—see. If you really want to know where you are, climb down to the road again."

"Yes," said Rollo.

"Walk seven miles straight ahead, turn seven times to the left, eight times to the right, and forty-nine times to neither, and you'll find out from a sign that stands along-side of the road just where you are. That's the best I can do for you, and I wouldn't have done that if you hadn't helped me up into this tree."

"Thank you," said Rollo. "But is *all* that necessary? Ca'n't you *tell* me where we are?"

"Oh, yes—I can," replied the Judge; "but I sha'n't because the evidence is not all before me. I may know a thing or two, but it wouldn't be judgely to tell it. Just you do what I tell you, and you'll find out all right."

And Rollo, like a good American citizen, followed strictly the instructions of the Judge.

He slid rapidly down the trunk of the birch-tree, regardless of its effect upon his trousers, reached the road, and followed its windings for at least seven miles, and without feeling the slightest weariness. Indeed, he seemed to glide along like an airship skimming over the clouds, as he expressed it afterward. He made the twists and the turns that the Judge had suggested, and, finally coming to a sort of embankment at one side of the highway, his eye fell upon a huge sign, bearing the words:—

EMBLEMLAND

"Emblemland, eh?" said Rollo. "That sounds rather interesting. I guess I'll investigate."

Which he immediately proceeded to do.

CHAPTER II

Rollo Meets Some Old Friends

*P*lunging his hands deep down into his pockets, and wondering all the while why in the course of his studies in geography he had never before come across such a place as Emblemland, Rollo walked on in the direction toward which the sign had pointed.

"I wonder what language the people speak here," he mused," and what kind of things they have to eat. I'm just a little bit hungry. Wouldn't mind a half-dozen cream-cakes and a glass of lemonade right now."

"We speak all languages, and we eat whatever we want," came a small voice from directly in front of him. Rollo, who had been walking with his head thrown back and his eyes upturned like Johnny-Look-in-the-Air, stopped short, and looked down.

"Why, hello," said he, as he espied the daintiest little Cupid imaginable standing in front of him. "Where did you come from?"

18

"I come from everywhere," replied the little Cupid. "But I live here mostly. Your name is Rollo, isn't it?"

"Yes," said Rollo. "How did you know?"

"They had you down in the newspapers as being among the prominent arrivals on the last boat in, and Captain Dolphin, who is a great favourite here, has told everybody that you are

19

the nicest passenger he ever had. It is true that he never had any others, but still it's a great compliment. He says everybody liked you from the Captain down to the Cabin-boy." Rollo laughed. He could see how that might very well be without making him the most popular creature in the world.

"I think he might have said good-bye to me, if he liked me so much," said Rollo. "He just splashed himself overboard, and left me in the lurch. It was a good lurch, but I don't think he was any too polite."

"He never says good-bye to anyone," explained Cupid. "He says he's sure to meet them again somewhere, so why should he? Good-bye is a sort of farewell forever term, you know."

"Well, I'll forgive him this time," said Rollo. "It was very good of him to bring me here, and I'm much obliged to him whether he said good-bye or not. What is Emblemland anyhow, Mr Cupid, and where is it?"

"Emblemland," Cupid explained, "is Emblemland, and it's here."

But I mean, who lives here and on what part of the map is it—Asia, Africa, America, or Europe?" persisted Rollo.

"It is the home of all the Emblems," said Cupid, "and it isn't on any map, because the Emblems are proud, and apt to be jealous of each other. You see, if it was on the map of Russia, the English Emblems wouldn't like it; and if it was on the map of France, the German Emblems would be vexed, and so on. For that reason we decided not to put it on any map. There's nothing like peace in the world, you know, and we've arranged matters here so that we have all we want of it all the time."

"Good idea," said Rollo. "But, I say, what's Emblems?"

"Why," said the little Cupid, "Emblems are signs and symbols. I'm an Emblem, because I am the symbol of love; Uncle Sam is the symbol of the United States, and John Bull is the symbol of England, and the Owl is the symbol of wisdom—they are all Emblems. See?"

"I'm getting it," said Rollo. "I'm the Emblem of starvation, because I'm awful hungry. Is that it?" Cupid laughed heartily. It was so very clear what Rollo was hinting.

"You're right," he said, "but we can soon fix that, and make you the Emblem of well-feddity. I'll take you down to the pump and fill you up."

"Pump?" cried Rollo, scornfully. "I didn't say I was thirsty. I don't want just a plain drink of water."

"Nobody said you did," retorted Cupid. "We have chicken-soup pumps, and lemonade pumps, and soda-water pumps, and sarsaparilla pumps—"

Rollo's mouth began to water as Cupid told of these marvellous things.

"I guess maybe that's the real reason you don't put this place on the map," the boy said. "You'd have the place overrun with small boys and tramps if they knew where to find a chicken-soup and sarsaparilla pump."

"It may be," said Cupid, quietly. "Maybe another reason is that we have candy mines here, too, where you can go with a pick and shovel and take out a bar of fine crisp taffy any time of day you happen to want it by just working an hour. See that field over there on the right?"

"The one with those big yellow daisies in it?" asked Rollo, as he gazed off in the direction Cupid had indicated.

"Yellow daisies!" laughed Cupid. "Those aren't yellow daisies; those are pumpkin pies."

"Mercy!" cried Rollo. "I'd like to spend a summer in this place."

"Who wouldn't," said Cupid, "with all the fine things we have here? Why, down in the Pudding Valley, just behind that big mountain over there, you'd find great lakes of custard, and apple trees bearing baked apples, and the mint bushes sprouting mince pies, and—well, I couldn't tell you of all the goodies we get here just for the gathering of them. If you'd like, you can run over to the pumpkin-pie field now—only don't eat too much," Cupid added with an odd twinkle in his eye.

"I should like nothing better," said Rollo, as he started off to investigate the delights of this strange and beautiful field.

But, alas! he was destined never to reach the field that sprouted custard pies instead of daisies. It seemed to jump about in a most exasperating fashion, now this way, now that, until Rollo gave up in despair. Try as he would, he could not seem to get any nearer to it.

"If that were my field, I'd anchor it!" he cried, impatiently, as he turned his back on it, and tried to make his way to his little friend Cupid again. This was equally hard, for, although Cupid was in plain sight, Rollo seemed wholly unable to retrace his steps.

"This surely must be the right road," he said to himself as he finally came to a narrow path that apparently led directly to where his friend was standing. "Yes—it—"

He did not finish his sentence, for, all on a sudden, his feet splashed in water. The path had ceased to be a path, and had turned into a swiftly running brook, on the other side of which Rollo was amazed to see a huge stork sitting with a book under his wing, staring at him intently out of two black, beady eyes, his great feet plunged into the rippling waters as far as they could go.

"Hello, Rollo," said the Stork. "Glad to see you again. You're a bigger boy now than you were the time I carried you to town."

"You? What?" demanded Rollo, slightly startled, for he never remembered having seen the Stork before.

"Yes, sir," said the Stork, pleasantly. "I'm the bird that did it. What did you think—think it was a canary-bird carried a ten-pounder like you all that distance?"

"I don't understand," said Rollo, very much mystified.

"What? Never heard of the Stork?" asked his new acquaintance. "Well, well, well! Where have you been all these days since I left you out on the piazza in response to a telegram from your father saying he'd like to have you home? I am the fellow that brings the babies to town, Rollo. I'm the baby Broker who deals in them, and the Expressman that delivers the goods. Here's my circular. I'll read it to you if you like." And the strange old bird took a piece of paper from his pocket, and, in response to Rollo's statement that he'd like to hear it very much, read the following lines to the wondering stranger:—

FALL ANNOUNCEMENT:
The Stork Baby Company, Unlimited.

Babies fat and babies thin.
Babies with a double chin.

Babies short and babies tall,
Babes that laugh and babes that squall.

Sleepy babies hit the sack,
Babies fond of ipecac.

Babies with a dimpled cheek,
Babies wrathy, babies meek.

Curly headed, chubby toes.
Sparkling eyes and snubby nose.

Babies sleepy, babies bright,
Babes that want to play all night.

Babies for the rich or poor—
I just leave them at the door

As the milkman does who brings
Cream and eggs and other things.

Leave them lying on the stoop
In a basket, with a whoop,

Just to let the people know
I am passing to and fro.

Anybody seeking one
Sends to me and it is done.

Girls or boys, it matters not
I've on hand an endless lot.

Glad to show them too to all
Patrons who would like to call.

When the Stork had finished reading his circular, he folded it up gravely and put it away in his book.

"So now you understand, I hope," he observed, "why I say I have seen you before. You came from my baby emporium, and it was I who packed you away in a wicker-basket and carried you to town. If you don't believe it, I'll show you my order-book."

Here the bird opened the volume that Rollo had noted under his wing.

"Let's see—the 4th of April, 1896. Wasn't that the date—the one you call your birthday?" he asked.

"It certainly was," said Rollo, staring at the old bird in amazement.

"I thought so," said the Stork, turning over the pages. "Yes; here it is: 'the 4th of April, 1896.—One Rollo delivered to Mr and Mrs John Periwinkle. All charges prepaid.' Signed and receipted for by John Periwinkle. Isn't that your father's signature?"

"It certainly looks like it," said Rollo, more startled than ever as he looked upon the page. "But—did I—did I come from Emblemland?" he asked.

"Oh, no," said the Stork. "Emblemland is only my place of residence. My factory is elsewhere; I ca'n't tell you where because it's a secret, and I don't want anybody but me to know it."

The Stork closed his book as he spoke, and shut both eyes for a moment.

"I'm enjoying this cool water on my claws," he said with a contented sigh. "I made a bad mistake while on my route last night, and I've been suffering from it ever since. I was taking a pair of twins down to some people in New York, and, feeling a little tired, I perched on an electric-light wire to rest—with the usual result. I think I got at least sixty-eight volts in each toe."

"Mercy!" cried Rollo.

"Shocking, wasn't it?" said the Stork. "It wasn't pleasant. I felt like a transatlantic cable before I got away, but I'm all right now. Hello, old man!"

These last words were addressed to a feeble-looking old fellow, with a scythe in one hand and an hourglass in the other, who appeared in an opening of the trees, and was gazing intently upon Rollo.

"Hello, Storky, who's your small friend?" asked the old fellow.

"This is Rollo Periwinkle," said the Stork.

"Oh, yes; he's the boy that doesn't pay much attention to me," said the stranger.

"The same," said the Stork. "Rollo, do you know who this gentleman is?"

"Yes, sir," said Rollo. "He's Rip Van Winkle."

The Stork roared with laughter, and the old gentleman grinned broadly.

"They know more about Rip Van Winkle than they do about me at his age," he said, kindly. "But I don't blame them. I'm pretty dull sometimes, and my companionship hangs heavy on their hands."

"Aren't you Mr Van Winkle, sir?" asked Rollo, respectfully.

"No, my son," said the old gentleman. "I am not Rip Van Winkle, nor anything like him save in appearance. He slept for twenty years, but I have never slept. I am the person they call Old Father Time. I am the man that was made for slaves, and I spend my days counting up my hours, and cutting down the future with my scythe. I lit the light of the sun way back in the beginning of things, and I invented darkness to soothe the tired eye. I set the ball we call the earth a-rolling, and have kept it going ever since. If you can catch me by the forelock, you can do almost anything you try. If you get behind me, you'll find yourself in all sorts of difficulties. If you keep abreast of me, you'll be ripe in wisdom and full of honours. If you are saving of me, you will find fortune; if you are wasteful of me, your life will be a failure. So you see. Master Periwinkle, I am a good person to take heed of. I don't know everything the way Mr Owl does, but what I do know is worth knowing. You don't happen to have a salted almond in your pocket, do you?"

"No," said Rollo, smiling at this droll request.

"Then I must be getting along," sighed the old gentleman. "The sun was five minutes late at Philadelphia yesterday morning, and everybody is complaining. I must run up there, and find out what the trouble is. Bye-bye."

And the strange old man passed on his way.

"He's a strange creature, is Old Father Time," said the Stork, as the old man vanished. "When he's pleasant, he's fine; when he's disagreeable, he's horrid, but he means well, and he never rests. I've known him to drag and I've known him to move so swiftly you'd think he was the lightning, and the queer thing about him is that, when you are enjoying pleasant company, he just flashes by, while, if your companions are disagreeable, he lingers and lingers and lingers around until you begin to think he'll never go."

"Too-Whoo-Too-Whoo-Too-Whoo!" cried a strident voice from the depths of the forest back of where the Stork was sitting.

"Mercy me!" said the Stork. "Doesn't that just prove- what I was saying? *It's school-time already*, and I was having such a nice little chat with you that I thought it was still hours off."

"School-time?" exclaimed Rollo. "I don't have to go to school here, do I?"

"Yes, sir," said the Stork. "It's one of our rules. Nobody can travel beyond the very edges of Emblemland without having passed an examination at the hands of Dr Owl. And why not? You have to pass a custom-house examination to get into the United States. Here it's only a school-house examination. It wo'n't take you long, and I wish you luck. Good-bye."

The Stork faded into a thin veil of mist, and Rollo, gazing after him as if to keep the kindly old bird in sight, was astonished to note right above his head, perched on the limb of a tree, a solemn-looking creature which he at once recognized as "The Bird of Wisdom".

CHAPTER III

The Examination and Some Other Things

"Well, my son," said the Owl, with a kindly glance at Rollo over the top of his glasses, "are you ready for your examination?"

"That depends on what you're going to ask me," said Rollo. "If you ask me questions I can answer, I guess maybe I'm ready, but if you're going into things like where was Julius Caesar born and who was Oliver Cromwell's aunt, I'm afraid I'm not quite ready."

"Good," said the Owl. "You've answered the first question correctly. How tall are you in miles?"

Rollo laughed. "I haven't the slightest idea, Mr Owl," he replied. "I never figured it out."

"That's right," said the Owl. "You are getting along famously. You are how many years and sixty-two days old?"

Rollo scratched his head. "I don't think I understand you, Mr Owl," he said.

"Right again," said the Owl, approvingly. "You really are a most exceptional student. Most boys of your age would have tried to guess at the answer in figures, with all the chances against their getting it right. I'll pass you in mathematics. Now, let's take up history. In what year did the Greeks capture Long Island?"

"I never heard that they did," said Rollo.

"Good. Neither did I," said the Owl. "I was afraid you'd say on the 5th of November, 1492. If you had, I should have had to keep you here until you'd got the right date, and, of course, as the thing never happened at all, you'd never have got away. Now, let's see—what is the next question? Who—ah—who succeeded Edward the Ninety-tooth as King of England?"

"Why," said Rollo, "there haven't been more than seven Edwards so far. How should I know that?"

"Magnificent—splendiferous," cried the Owl. "I never knew a finer examination in history; but there is one more question, Rollo, and you must think carefully before you venture upon your answer. What King of France was it who said, 'After me the deluge'? Don't answer too hastily now. Take your time."

"I don't know," said Rollo. "Was it Noah?"

"Maybe it was—sounds like him, doesn't it!" said the Owl, scratching his head. "I really don't know myself. I was in hopes you'd tell me; but I'll give you ten on the question, anyhow, and pass you in history. You are a wonderfully well-informed boy. I find we must go back to mathematics for a moment. The government insists upon this question, and I forgot to ask it. If seven boys have seven bananas and four apples apiece at ten o'clock in the morning on the thirtieth of February, how many peaches will they have left at six o'clock at night on the sixteenth day of April after a walk of ninety-eight miles, four rods, and six furlongs, having eaten five pounds of beefsteak, a bushel of potatoes, and fourteen lemon-pies at the end of every ninth mile?"

"There isn't any thirtieth of February," said Rollo.

"Exactly right," said the Owl. "We ca'n't catch you on mathematics. Now for Astronomy. What is the average distance from the earth to the sun, the moon, the dipper, and the top of Mount Washington?"

"I don't know anything about astronomy," said Rollo.

"Splendid," said the Owl. "You are really the finest student I have had yet. When does the sun rise?"

"In the morning," said Rollo.

"But at what time?" asked the Owl, severely.

"Oh—about dawn," said Rollo.

"Right," said the Owl. "And the moon?"

"Mostly at night," said Rollo.

"Right again," said the Owl. "You know enough about astronomy to get along. And now for your languages. What language do the Germans speak?"

"It depends," said Rollo, "on where they are. We have a German carpenter at our house sometimes who tries to speak English."

"What do you know about Latin?"

"Nothing," said Rollo.

"And what is French for 'I don't care for any breakfast this morning'?"

"I don't know," said Rollo. "I never felt that way in any language."

"You are all right on languages," observed the Owl. "You have passed a perfect examination. I'll mark you 100. And now, we'll finish up with a test of your grammar. Suppose I should say 'I bes a monkey', instead of 'I am a monkey'. What would you say?"

"I should say that you were wrong," Rollo answered, "because you are an Owl."

"Just a plain Owl?" asked the Owl, eying Rollo anxiously.

"No," said Rollo. "A very interesting Owl."

"You're a very clever boy," said the Owl, with a good-natured smile, "and you may consider yourself free to enter Emblemland, and without further examination."

Here the queer old bird came down off the limb of the tree, and shook hands very pleasantly with the little traveller.

"I'm glad to meet you," he said, as he polished off his glasses and rubbed up his hat. "You know so little, and are so perfectly willing to confess it. My experience with boys has been that they pretend to know a lot without knowing half as much as you and I don't, who can multiply six by four or seven by eight, and come within ten or twelve of the correct answer. Of course, you understand that I don't know so very much myself off-hand, but I've got it all here," he added, tapping his book. "It's all right down in print in this book: 243 times 967, and who discovered Alaska, and things like that. If there's anything worth knowing, I can find it out by looking in this book. Only the other day a man came to me and said how many automobiles are sixteen horses multiplied by thirteen sets of harness. I didn't know, of course. But I looked in this book, and answered 'twenty-eight', and you should have seen how he looked when he walked away. Mighty cheap, I can tell you. He thought he had me.

> "I don't know all there is to know,
> But I'm aware that snow is snow.
> I do not have to guess to say
> That sunshine makes a pleasant day.
> It does not take me long to state
> That four and six are two plus eight;
> That seven apples minus three
> Leave one more than is good for me;
> That sixty multiplied by two
> Is quite an easy sum to do;

That William called the Conqueror
Discovered not Americor;
That Louis Tenth, the King of France,
Was not the man who studied ants;
That old Columbus sailed the sea
And ran against Amerikee;
That Caesar was a splendid swell
Who wrote in Latin mighty well;
That it is always well to look
Before you answer, in a book
To find out if you really know
That this and that are so and so.

"In other words, Rollo, never answer a question without finding out beforehand that you know what you are talking about."

Rollo was about to tell the Owl that he thought he was very wise indeed when he caught sight of two smiling old gentlemen walking along the road, chatting and laughing together as if they were brothers—which, as it turned out, they were.

"There go the twins," said the Owl, with a twinkle in his eye: "Uncle Sam and Johnny Bull. They're a great pair, taking them by and large. Uncle Sam is tall and thin and not as dressy as he might be, and Johnny Bull is short and stumpy and looks as if he had always plenty to eat, but they're twins just the same. Same mother and father, and no differences at all except in their boats. Sam thinks his is the best and proves it, and John thinks his is the best and comes near proving it. Year in and year out, they sail their little craft down in the lake here—"

"Lake?" said Rollo.

"Well—pond, then," said the Owl. "It seems big enough sometimes to be called a lake, but it isn't much more than a

34

pond after all, and Sammy lives on one side and Johnny on the other."

"I thought you meant an ocean," said Rollo.

"Oh, well, suppose I did?" said the Owl. "What's an ocean between friends? A pond is an ocean to an ant, and a lake is an ocean to a mouse. Why shouldn't an ocean be a lake or a pond to a man? It's nothing more than a lake multiplied by a thousand, and a man is an ant multiplied by twenty thousand. Really those two chaps are next-door neighbours, though they live over three thousand miles apart. It wouldn't take much to have them living in the same house together if it wasn't for their little boats."

"They seem to be having a good time together," said Rollo, as he gazed after the retreating figures.

"Well, why shouldn't they?" demanded the Owl. "They haven't anything to quarrel about—now. They used to have, but they fought it all out, which is a good thing to do whether you like fighting or not. Get rid of your fighting as quick as you can, say I. And that's just what Uncle Sam and Johnny Bull have done."

A roar of laughter from the latter interrupted the Owl's observations.

"Uncle Sam has just cracked one of his jokes," said the Owl. "Hey! Sammy—what you laughing at? Here's a young American visitor who wouldn't mind smiling a bit himself."

"Haven't got time to stop now," Uncle Sam called back. "Tell him I'll meet him at the boat-race next fall. I'll—be—on—the—first—yacht—over—the—line."

And with this the two old fellows disappeared around the turn.

"And now, my dear Rollo," said the Owl, "I must go back to my perch and study up. There's a Chinaman coming over to-night, and I don't know enough Chinese to ask him if he thinks it will rain to-morrow. Good-bye, and good luck to you."

Rollo bade his wise friend farewell, and passed up the road thinking that, considering how much he really knew, the Owl was a very charming person.

"Wasn't a bit stuck-up," he said, "like some other school-teachers I've met. I wouldn't mind going to school if they were all like him."

> *"Tra-la-la-la,*
> *Trol-lolley-car,*
> *Tooral-li-ooral-o-tooral-i-ay!"*

came a happy little voice from far up the road. Evidently somebody, somewhere, was enjoying himself hugely, and Rollo began to run in order to discover who and what the singer was as soon as possible. He had not gone two hundred yards when, directly in the road before him, standing on its head and wriggling a pair of funny little legs in the air, was the drollest little figure imaginable.

"Looks like a Football with legs," said Rollo, aloud.

"That's just what I be," returned the little chap. "Kick me quick," he added. "I'm just dying to be kicked."

"Oh, no!" said Rollo. "I'm afraid I should hurt you."

"Hurt me? Not a bit of it. Why, it wouldn't hurt me if a house fell on me. Go on—give me a kick. I just love it," said the Football.

"Very well," said Rollo. "If you insist, I'll do it, but it strikes me as a very queer way to begin an acquaintance." And he hauled back his leg and kicked the Football squarely in the middle of its back, and as hard as he knew how.

"Sus-spul-lendid!" cried the Football, gleefully, as he sailed off through the air—by which I presume he meant *splendid*. "You've evidently practised at this business before," he continued, as, after turning a dozen or more somersaults in the air, he came bounding back to earth again.

"Yes," said Rollo. "I'm halfback and quarterback and centre-rush on our school eleven."

"All those?" asked the Football.

"Yes," said Rollo. "You see, our eleven has only got five boys on it."

"Too bad. You get beaten all the time, I suppose," said the Football.

"Oh, no, indeed," said Rollo. "We always win. None of the other elevens have more than four. Doesn't it hurt to be kicked?"

"Of course not," said the Football. "Does it hurt you to be kissed?"

"No," said Rollo.

"Well, it's the same way with me when I'm kicked. I'd rather be kicked than kissed any day. You ca'n't imagine how delightful it is to rise up from the toe of a really good player and go soaring off into the emptyryrean, as the Greek Professor calls it, like an airship. That Mr Santy Dumont isn't in it with me when it comes to the joy of making a goal from the field."

"But doesn't it jar you when you come down?" Rollo asked.

"Not a bit—that's great fun, too; and the harder the landing-place, the better I like it," said the Football. "I wrote a poem about it once. Let's see if I can remember how the thing went. It's called *'The Song of the Football'*:—

> *"I love the cool, crisp autumn days*
> *When Footballs come in style,*
> *For then you see I wear the bays*
> *And life is all a smile.*
>
> *"I love it when the quarterback*
> *Swings back his good right leg*
> *And gives me such a fearful crack*
> *'Twould smash the toughest egg.*
>
> *"I love it when I'm underneath*
> *Some ten or twenty men*
> *Who're fighting with both nails and teeth*
> *To catch me up again.*
>
> *"I love to sail between the posts*
> *And win the festive goal,*
> *And when I hear the cheering hosts*
> *'Tis nectar to my soul.*
>
> *"I love to bump my nose upon*
> *The hard and frozen earth;*
> *And when I'm jumped on by a ton*
> *Of men I roar with mirth.*

"I even like it when I fall
With dull and sickening thud
In quick response to duty's call
Into the oozy mud.

"So keep your soft caresses for
The folks that like them best.
For me the buffet on the jaw.
The whack upon the chest.

"I'll naught of kisses, nor of soft
Endearments—no, not I,
But joyously will soar aloft
When kicked upon the eye."

"Rather curious taste, though," said Rollo.

"Not for a football," replied the Football. "If I were a man, I probably wouldn't like having twenty-two men pushing my face into the earth, and stamping all over my spine, and gouging their knees into my stomach, but, as a football, I cannot only stand it, but like it better than eating. Kick me again, will you?"

"With pleasure," said Rollo, and he gave his queer little friend the kind of kick that his father used to complain about when Rollo, in his dreams, let out both legs at once and sent his poor old daddy out of the other side of the bed on to the floor.

The Football had barely had time to get back to earth again, when a frightful racket from overhead fell upon Rollo's ears and startled him very much.

"Whoa! Pegasus—whoa-up there!" cried a sweet silvery voice from way above him, and then, with a crash before him on the road, down came a winged horse, stumbling upon his knees, and tossing over his head a pretty little rider whom

Rollo immediately recognized as his old friend Puck. Rollo ran to his assistance as soon as he had recovered from his surprise.

"I hope you aren't hurt," he cried.

"Not in the slightest," said Puck. "Peggy is a hard horse to ride, but I'm getting used to him. He's thrown me seven times already this morning."

"But you landed on your head," cried Rollo.

"I know," said Puck. "I always do. That's why I wear this beaver hat. It breaks my fall, you see. It's bad for the hat, but saves my head. And, now, are you ready? I have come to escort you into the land of the Jokers."

"Indeed, I am," said Rollo.

"All right," said Puck, "get aboard. Good-bye, Footy," he added, turning to the Football. "I'd be glad to have you come along too, but I know you are busy."

"Yes, thank you," returned the Football. "I'm going over to New Haven this afternoon. The Yale eleven have got a lot of new kicks they want to try, and they've given me the refusal of the lot. I wouldn't miss it for a farm. Good-bye."

The little chap went bounding merrily down the road, and Rollo, mounting Pegasus behind Puck, soon found himself enjoying a most delightful horseback ride through the air.

CHAPTER IV

By Pegasus
to Joker's Town

"Isn't this perfectly gorgeous!" cried Rollo, as Pegasus, flapping his wings vigorously, rose high into the heavens, and, as if to show off all his many fine qualities, leaped over clouds as if they were so many hurdles, and cleared sundry steeples and high-roofed buildings at a bound.

"He's a great old horse," said Puck. "But he's tricky—tricky as an automobile. Aren't you, Peg?"

Pegasus whisked his tail and, resting on his wings for a moment, began to try to show how tricky he was by swooping down toward the earth so rapidly that Rollo was truly alarmed, yet when he seemed about to come crashing down to the hard surface of a highway, rising again like a soaring bird until the world seemed hardly more than a tiny speck in the vast blue, so far beneath them had it been left.

"He likes to play all sorts of pranks when he gets way up here, and you have to watch him pretty carefully," Puck continued. "He isn't vicious, but he is skittish, and it's no

uncommon thing, when he finds himself right over a body of water or some soft, mushy spot in the turf, to throw his rider clean over his head down to a ducking, or something else uncomfortable. It takes a mighty experienced poet to ride him."

"You seem to do pretty well," said Rollo.

"Of course," Puck returned, "because I am a mighty experienced poet. I have been in the joke and poetry business for years and years. I can write a sonnet with my eyes shut, and, when it comes to jokes, I can crack three at a time without even thinking about it."

"I wish you'd crack a few for me now," said Rollo.

"Oh, I shouldn't dare, way up here," Puck answered. "You'll have all you can do hanging on without my making you laugh. Wait until we get to Joker's Town, and you'll get all the jokes you want. They serve them at meals there."

Rollo immediately perceived the wisdom of Puck's statement, for the words were hardly out of his mouth when Pegasus, seeing a small boy's kite directly in front of him, pretended to be frightened at it, and shied violently. Both riders were unseated, Rollo wholly so. However, he managed to hold on to Puck, who, in some way, in turn managed to hold on to Pegasus so that no harm was done to anyone. With Puck's assistance, he scrambled back into his place again, and put his whole attention upon the ticklish business of holding on tight.

After riding a few moments in silence, Rollo perceived a great black rain-cloud ahead of him, and it was evident that, if they passed under it, they would be drenched.

"We're going to have a storm, I guess," he said. "Wouldn't we better go down and get under cover?"

"We'll do better than that," said Puck. "We'll keep up in the sunshine, and avoid the wetting altogether." Tapping Pegasus lightly on the side with his whip, which was nothing else than a stylus almost as big as himself, Puck indicated to the winged steed that he wished him to go over instead of under the rain-cloud, and Pegasus, with a whinny of delight—for he was fond of flying high—turned his snorting nostrils upward, and was soon miles and miles above the cloud that was drenching all beneath it. It was a peculiar experience for Rollo to find himself so far up above the world, and once or twice it made him dizzy, but the excitement of it all was so great that not for an instant did he wish himself back on the road again.

"It's better than an airship, isn't it?" he said, catching his breath at the magnificence of the view that was to be had from this enormous height.

"Well, I should say so," said Puck. "Just as much better as a real live horse is better than an automobile. These airships aren't much good, and, if they get caught in a heavy wind, there's no telling where they'll bring up; and, if they break down—well, it's good-bye, all. There was one of them up here a week ago got caught in a hurricane, and was blown all the way out to the Great Dipper, where it was wrecked, and now the people who were aboard of her don't know how on earth they are ever going to get back again."

"Could you drive Pegasus that far?" asked Rollo.

"Yes, but it's a long pull for a horse," said Puck. "It's an up-hill fly all the way. Coming back, it's fine, because all he has to do is to spread his wings and soar downward, but we seldom do it because getting there tires him so. If there were any hotels or stables of any kind on the way out, where we could stop and rest, it would be different. Hey there, Pegasus, whoa! What's the matter with you, anyhow?"

The animal began to plunge and rear, and then he started at a terrible rate of speed across the sky.

"He—he isn't running away, is he?" asked Rollo, anxiously.

"That's just what he is doing," said Puck. "And all we can do is to let him run. There's nothing he can run into, and, as long as we can keep our seats, we are all right."

Rollo's hair streamed out behind him, so rapidly were they moving, and the crisp air whistled in his ears as the runaway steed plunged madly ahead.

"D–does he do th–this often?" stammered Rollo, grabbing his hat from his head in order not to lose it.

"Frequently," said Puck. "He doesn't like lightning, and, coming by that last cloud, he stepped into an electric current. Don't worry, though. We'll be all right as soon as his breath begins to give out. Running away is an excellent cure for a runaway horse, if you only keep him at it."

It fortunately turned out as Puck had said. Pegasus ran on and on for fifteen or twenty minutes—it seemed as many weeks to Rollo—and then his strength began to give out, and his breath came and went in " short pants", as Puck expressed it, "like a small boy". His ears drooped, and then his legs stopped. His wings were outstretched to the fulness of their length, and the three travellers of the air, riders and horse, dropped gently to earth again.

"Good!" said Puck, as they alighted before a huge castle-wall. "Here we are at last. This, Rollo, is the entrance to the far-famed Joker's Town, and there comes one of the guardians out to meet us."

Rollo looked ahead of him, and there, sure enough, clad in brilliant armour, riding a magnificent horse, and holding his lance gracefully in his hand, was a handsome knight. Off to the right of the castle and within the walls was a huge broad building, a single story in height, and on the left was a beautiful pagoda of great size.

"That's the Joke Foundry at the right," said Puck, in a low whisper to Rollo. "And the building on the left is the Comic Poetry Mill."

"And who is the Knight on horseback?" asked Rollo.

"That is Life," said Puck, "or, rather, a part of Life's staff. He is the fellow that does the fighting outside, while Life himself, a chubby little fatling Cupid, stays quietly inside and coins smiles for the million."

Rollo was properly impressed by the magnificence of all that lay before him, for Joker's Town was one of the most brilliant cities in the world. It has to be kept bright always, for it would never do were it to become dull and grimy.

"Come," said Puck. "Don't stand here staring at Life all day. There's a lot to be seen inside the gates, and you haven't a minute too much time."

The little couple walked on, and, as they passed the Knight, he saluted Rollo as if he were a general.

"Has the young man passed his examinations yet?" he asked of Puck.

"Got a hundred per cent, in every one of them," Puck answered.

"Does he know the difference between a joke and a ton of coal?" asked Life.

"Certainly I do," said Rollo. "I knew that before I came here. Papa told me once that the difference between a ton of coal and a joke depended on the joke, and whether it would burn or not. A good many jokes are heavy as a ton of coal, but don't give out so much heat."

"You're all right, young man," said Life's Herald. "Pass in, and welcome to the ranks. Better take him to the Joke

Foundry first, Pucky," the Herald added. "They are busy as bees to-day."

So Rollo was taken into the Joke Foundry, where he was introduced to a pleasant little person whom he immediately recognized as Mr Punch.

"Mr Punch, Rollo," Puck said, as he introduced the visitor, "is the oldest joker in the business, and we have made him President of the Joke Trust, as well as Mayor of Joker's Town."

"Glad to meet you, Mr Punch," said Rollo. "I've read lots of your jokes lots of times."

"Aha!" cried Mr Punch, turning triumphantly to Puck. "See that? Now, who was right? I said my jokes were read, and you said they were grey."

"Well, I never said they were green," said Puck. Mr Punch laughed.

"They are all down on me, Rollo," he said, and, entirely as if he didn't mind it at all, "because I have a fondness for *old* jokes. These other chaps want new ones all the time, and, just because I insist upon the proper respect due to old age, they say I am old-fashioned. Ca'n't a boy be fond of his father without wanting to throw his grandfather out of the window, is the way I put it."

"I like new jokes myself," said Rollo.

"Of course you do," said Mr Punch. "Who doesn't? I do, myself. But you aren't going back on the old friends that made you laugh once, are you? I tell you, my boy, I judge people nowadays by the way in which they treat old jokes. If they receive them reverently, and with a kindly smile as much as to say, 'Oh, indeed, I remember you—you drove out my tears once, and gave me a jolly smile in place of them; I'm glad to see you again,' I like them. It shows that they are grateful to an old servitor who helped them over an unhappy moment. And I'd trust those people anywhere. But the fellow that forgets all the old joke has done for him, and who cries out, 'Get out of here, you old chestnut,' I haven't any use for him at all. As the poet said:—

> *"It isn't what you are, old joke,*
> *That makes me smile at you.*
> *'Tis not new laughter you invoke.*
> *But mirth that's just as true.*

> *"The welcome I accord to-day*
> *Is hearty in good truth*
> *As that of men grown old and grey*
> *To friends they knew in youth.*

> *"For you, the joke of other times,*
> *That helped when I was blue*
> *To set in tune the jangled chimes*
> *That filled my soul with rue.*

> *"I have a welcome warm and sweet*
> *To make your pulses start,*
> *And offer you a soft retreat*
> *Here in my grateful heart."*

Mr Punch's voice grew husky as he recited his little poem, and even Rollo's eyes wet up a trifle as he listened.

Puck laughed as he noted how touched Rollo was, but he patted the boy on the shoulder as he did so.

"It's all right, my lad," he said. "Mr Punch is right. The old joke should always be made to feel that it is welcome, but our old neighbour, Punch, here doesn't content himself with providing them with an asylum—he keeps them working. All I say is, give the old joke a rest."

"Exercise is good for them," said Mr Punch, shortly. "They seem fresher for it, and I keep them exercised. That's all. Now, suppose we take Rollo through the foundry."

This was done in short order, and Rollo saw for the first time how jokes were made. He saw thousands of solemn-looking workmen take a handful of words out of a great big vat that was labelled:

> THE VOCABULARY.
> DO NOT SPILL THE WORDS ON
> THE FLOOR.

These they mixed with a dark liquid substance that looked like ink—and which, in fact, was ink—until the mixture became thick as a rather heavy paste, which they worked over and over again with their hands until it in turn resembled an idea. This was put aside until it had hardened like the crust of a loaf of bread, and was then sent off to be pointed. The pointing operation consisted in infusing into the mass a sharper word, which made all the others appear to mean something entirely different from what they had ever meant before, after which the whole thing was sent to the polishing-room, and there scoured and brushed and turned and twisted until it was as brilliantly bright as shining gold. The joke was then supposed to be finished, and was stored away in the delivery-room to be sent out to the customers who patronized the great industry of Joker's Town. I have not the time nor the space to tell you of all that Rollo saw in that wonderful factory. How he watched them for a half hour making Puns; how he visited the place where all the funny tricks the clowns in the circuses do were got up by retired clowns of all ages; how he saw the place where broken jokes were repaired, and old ones made over so that they seemed almost new. Nor is there room here for a full account of the wonderful Joke Museum, where Rollo saw, in a long row of glass cases, the two oldest jokes in the world—the two that Noah had on the Ark with him—and all the other joke curiosities of the day, from those of ancient Greece and Egypt down to a whole case full of jests that George Washington carried with him through the War of the Revolution. It was a wonderful exhibit, and Rollo would have been glad to stay within doors looking at it all day, but word came that the Tournament was about to begin, when the Knight of Life was to combat with the Emblem of the Wicked Joke, a huge bat-shaped creature that went about making fun of woe and misery; making people laugh at suffering, not sympathize with sufferers; causing trouble with his mean practical jokes; the Emblem that invented the jests that bring sorrow to people, pain to the meek and lowly.

"We mustn't miss that," said Mr Punch, "for it is going to be a great fight."

But Mr Punch was mistaken, for the minute Life's Knight appeared in the arena, his helmet visor down, his shield buckled fast to his arm and his lance poised to give battle, with an unearthly yell of fear and rage, the Wicked Jester turned and fled like the coward that he was, and just as he always does. There was no fight in him.

A great cheer went up from the multitude as Life routed his adversary, and the sun, which had been peeping timidly from behind a cloud as if in fear of the result, now came out, full-faced and golden, and smiled down upon the happy, clean, and wholesome Joker's Town.

"I'm glad he beat him," said Rollo, as, later, he and Mr Punch strolled along together through a neighbouring wood. "If there is anything I dislike in the world, it's a mean joke."

"Me, too," said Mr Punch. "I'd rather have a bad one that's kindly than the meanest mean joke in the world. And now, Rollo, come along with me. The Judge and I are going to read our jokes aloud to the Crocodile. He's been shedding tears for centuries, and we've bet Puck and Life a shad dinner against a waste-basket that we can make him laugh."

"How about the Comic Poetry Mill?" asked Rollo.

"Oh, that's the Joke Foundry all over again," Mr Punch answered. "They just saw the jokes up into lines of equal length, and put a capital letter at one end and a rhyme at the other end of each line. The process of manufacture is exactly the same."

"Very well, then," said Rollo. "I'll go with you, and see you and the Judge try your jokes on the Crocodile."

And the two passed down through the wood together.

CHAPTER V

The Jesters
and the Crocodile

"What is the Crocodile doing in Emblemland?" asked Rollo, as he and Mr Punch walked along.

"Shedding tears, of course," said Mr Punch. "That's all he's good for, though you'd think otherwise to look at his mouth. It is the most curious thing in the world that a creature, with a mouth just made for smiles as a crocodile's is, should never laugh. I measured his mouth only last Tuesday, and from jowl to jowl it's five feet seven inches as it stands. What a gorgeous smile that would make stretched, eh?"

"Splendid," said Rollo.

"And all he does is shed tears! It's perfectly disgusting. A creature that should be the emblem of mirth is nothing but a picture of woe," Mr Punch growled on.

"Haven't you tried to reform him?" asked Rollo.

"Reform him?" demanded Mr Punch. "Reform a crocodile? Never. He's too thick-skinned, if you know what that means."

"I don't," said Rollo.

"Well, it means that there's no way of prodding him so that it will hurt," explained Mr Punch. "You ca'n't spank him hard enough to make any impression on his mind, and he hasn't enough brains to be reached by argument. You could talk to him all day, trying to prove to him that black was black, and, if he'd set his mind on it that it was pink or yellow or green, you couldn't move him. It's exasperating. He observed only the other night that he didn't see why two and two couldn't make seven just as easy as four, and everyone of us took a hand at showing him why it was so, and all we could get out of him was: 'Nonsense. It's only a notion. Two and two could make ninety-seven if it wanted to.' What are you going to do with a fellow that talks that way?"

"How did he pass his examinations getting into Emblemland?" asked Rollo.

"Oh, Dr Owl said his ignorance was so perfect he thought he ought to pass—said he was a regular Napoleon of Misinformation. So they let him in. But as for reforming him—well, they turned out a rhyme up at the Comic Poetry Mill the other day on that very subject. As I remember it, it ran this way:—

"You ca'n't reform an Elephant
Because he keeps his sentiment
Far out of reach, deep down within
A six-inch layer tough of skin.
And as for the Rhinoceros
He's also very hard to boss,
Because his hide's so very thick
You couldn't dent it with a pick.
Then there's the Alligator, too,
Whose flesh is seven inches through.
You'll prod him hard as e'er you like
With bowie-knife or marlin-spike
And never get a single squeal—

His epiderm is hard as steel!
And so with Mr Crocodile,
Punch, prod, and pinch him all the while
And he would never, never know
Unless somebody told him so,
And even then he'd wink his eyes
And say he thought the prods were flies.
Your chances would be better far
If you reformed a trolley-car.

He's hopeless."

"I don't believe you can make him laugh if he's as bad as all that," said Rollo.

"Oh, I don't know about that," Mr Punch answered. "The Judge and I have made harder cases than the Crocodile laugh. I went into the British Museum once, and put in an hour cracking jokes with the Mummies up in the Egyptian room, and at the end of twenty minutes I had them all in convulsions. And the Judge tells me that two winters ago, down in New York, he got a laugh out of the bronze statue of Shakespeare up in Central Park. Fellows that can do that sort of thing needn't have any fear of a Crocodile."

"Maybe, if you get him laughing just once instead of crying, he'll like it so much better that he'll take to laughter instead of to tears hereafter," suggested Rollo.

"Maybe," said Mr Punch. "It wo'n't do any harm to try anyhow, and, if we succeed, it will be a great thing for us Jokers, I tell you. If the Crocodile put on a smiling face with that mouth of his, it would be a splendid advertisement for my jokes. And, by the way, do you hear that roaring sound?"

"Like a cataract?" said Rollo, listening intently.

"Yes," said Mr Punch, "only it isn't a *cat*aract It's more what you might call a *crocodil*aract. It's him, and the rushing waters you hear are the tears he's shedding coursing down his nose and cheeks."

"Mercy, what a damp person he must be," said Rollo. "May I see him?"

"Certainly," said Mr Punch. "Run ahead just beyond the edge of the wood, and you'll find him sitting on a bank. Meanwhile, I'll find the Judge."

Rollo started along, while Mr Punch, leaving the road, disappeared into the depths of the forest. The lad had not walked far when he came to an opening in the trees, and found himself at last out of the wood, and in a somewhat barren and rocky country.

Forty yards away, as Mr Punch had said, seated upon an embankment at one side of the road, was the Crocodile, crying as if his heart would break. The tears simply gushed from his eyes like the water from a faucet with an unusually heavy pressure on.

"Poor old fellow," said Rollo, as he gazed upon the pathetic sight. "How he must suffer!"

"Nothing of the sort," retorted the Crocodile, angrily. "I'm not a poor old fellow at all. I'm a rich old fellow, and I never suffered in all my life."

"Then what are you crying about?" demanded Rollo.

"Because I like to," said the Crocodile. "Why do you eat buckwheat cakes?

"Why do you dote on apple-pie?
Why do you dote on jam?
Why are you fond of hard-boiled eggs
Washed down with a slice of ham?

"Why do you smile till your ears fall in?
Why do you jump with glee,
When the waitress brings a plate of cakes
For your Sunday evening tea?"

"Because they're good, and I like them," said Rollo.

"Well, I cry for the same reason. Weeping is tarts to me. Wo'n't you join me in a good cry?" asked the Crocodile.

Rollo laughed. "I don't care for crying myself," said he, "unless I've got something to cry about."

"What utter, utter nonsense," groaned the Crocodile. "Having something to cry about spoils all the fun of it. As my poem has it:—

> "'Tis better far to cry for fun
>   Than 'tis to weep for woe—
> I found that out e'er I begun,
>   And hence I ought to know.
>
> "To cry for fun means that your tears
>   Give pleasure as they fall,
> While if you cry for woe, my dears,
>   It ain't no fun at all.
>
> "For don't you see that all the fun
>   That comes from weeping thus
> Is absolutely spoiled and done
>   Because you're in a muss?

"Furthermore, moreover, likewise, and withal, if you cry for nothing, you are apt to get it—"

Get what?" queried Rollo.

"Nothing," snuffled the Crocodile. "Whereas, if you cry for something, the chances are that you wo'n't. Hence, it is clear that you are a very foolish young man to wait for something to cry about before plunging in and having a good weep."

"But do you never laugh?" asked Rollo.

"Laugh! Why should I laugh? What at? When, where, and why?" demanded the Crocodile.

"What's the good of laughing when you can cry? No, sir. I leave laughing to babies. It's all right for them, for they don't know any better, but for a full-grown, sensible Crocodile laughing is very undignified business."

"But don't you ever laugh at Mr Punch's jokes?" Rollo asked.

"Of course not," cried the Crocodile, indignantly. "Laugh at Mr Punch's jokes? Pretty question to ask. Why, he's a friend of mine, Mr Punch is. Jokes are his business, and I should be very rude indeed if I laughed at them.

> *"Suppose you were a grocery man,*
> *And I dropped in your store,*
> *And every time you sold some tea*
> *I burst into a roar?*
>
> *"Suppose you drove a hansom cab*
> *And every time you passed*
> *I doubled up and shrieked as if*
> *That moment was my last?*
>
> *"Suppose you ran a peanut stand*
> *Would you not think it queer*
> *If every time I looked at it*
> *I grinned from ear to ear?*
>
> *"Suppose you made old furniture,*
> *What would you think of me,*
> *If I called in to laugh at it*
> *With wild hilarity?*
>
> *"Suppose you were a clergyman,*
> *Whose sermons all were strong.*
> *And every time you preached I laughed,*
> *Would you not think it wrong?"*

"Of course I would," said Rollo. "But, somehow or other, jokes are different."

"They're just as hard work as selling peanuts," said the Crocodile. "And, after Mr Punch has worked honestly and hard for days and days making a joke, it would be extremely unfriendly of me to laugh at it."

Rollo wanted very much to laugh himself at the strange old creature, but he did not quite dare to after these remarks, so he stood and gazed at him silently for a few minutes.

"Do you live here all the year round?" he asked, finally, since the Crocodile showed no signs of beginning the conversation anew.

"Here and in Egypt," the Crocodile answered. "I'm the Emblem of the Nile," he added, as he burst forth into the following ditty:—

> *"Oh, the Emblem of the Nile*
> *Is the old Crocodile*
> *Who is never known to smile,*
> *But is weeping all the while,*
> *In the very latest style—*
> *And so on for a mile."*

"Never go travelling, eh?" said Rollo.

"Haven't yet," said the Crocodile. "I'm too busy Embleming. When I die, if I ever do, maybe I'll go travelling then."

"When you die?" cried Rollo, in amazement.

"Certainly," replied the Crocodile. "That's the chief occupation of defunct Crocodiles and Alligators. They skin us, and make travelling-bags of us, and in that way we go all over. I had a brother once named Jimmie, and, when he died, he went all over the world as a sole-leather trunk. And he made a mighty good one, too. I saw him once, five years after he died, on a baggage-wagon up in Cairo, just chock-full of books,

and opera hats, and pants and things, and, when they threw
him off the top of the wagon down on the sidewalk, it never
even scratched him. Jimmy was the hardest crocodile I ever
saw, and the man who had him made over into a trunk told a
friend of mine that he wouldn't part with him for seven
dollars—and that was a time when there wasn't more than
eight dollars in all the world." And the speaker's tears burst
forth with redoubled force and quantity.

"Dear me!" thought Rollo. "Mr Punch and the Judge will
have a hard time with him"—an idea which the events that
now followed showed to be wholly correct. The Crocodile had
hardly finished his pathetic references to his departed brother
when Mr Punch came up, accompanied by a smiling old fellow,
with a twinkling eye, whom Rollo immediately recognized as
his first acquaintance in Emblemland, the gentleman he had
assisted in climbing the tree down by the beach some moments
after he landed.

"How-d'ye-do again, Rollo," he said, genially. "I see you got here all right."

"Yes, thank you," said Rollo.

"And here is dear old Crocky, too," observed the Judge, turning to the Crocodile, who received him with comparative amiability. "Still weeping?" asked the Judge.

"Oh, of course not," retorted the Crocodile. "I'm sawing wood."

"Fair joke that," said Mr Punch.

"What?" roared the Crocodile. "A joke—a remark of mine a joke? Come, come, Mr Punch. You mustn't try to provoke me."

"A thousand apologies," began Mr Punch.

"One will be enough," snapped the Crocodile. "I haven't got time to listen to a thousand. What are you fellows up to to-day?"

"Mr Punch and I want to read some of our jokes to you," said the Judge. "Hope you don't object?"

"Gracious," said the Crocodile. "Again?"

"No—not again," returned Mr Punch. "These are all entirely new ones."

"I think I could stand it better," said the Crocodile, with a hysterical sob, "if you gave me some of the old ones."

"We'll mix them," said Mr Punch. "Are you ready?"

"I suppose so," answered the Crocodile, wearily. "But do it up as rapidly as you can, for I'm very tired this morning. I've just been talking to this boy Rollo, and he's such an ignoramus!"

"Ho!" said Rollo. "I know more in my little finger than you do in a week."

"That may be," said the Crocodile. "But you keep what you know in your little finger instead of in your head, where it might be of some use to someone. But go ahead, gentlemen. I'm ready."

Whereupon the Crocodile settled wearily back upon the bank, folded his forelegs over his chest, and continued to weep while Messrs. Punch and Judge opened their books and began.

"Here's a riddle," said Mr Punch. "And it's a mighty good one, too. What's the difference between an old-fashioned timepiece and a certain carnivorous lizard that doesn't know enough to go in when it rains?"

"That sounds juicy," said the Judge.

"I give it up," said Rollo.

"Fire ahead," sighed the Crocodile. "What is the difference?"

"One is a sun-dile and the other's a crocodile," answered Mr Punch, bursting forth into shouts of laughter.

But the Crocodile was apparently not of the same mind, for his only response was an extra gallon of tears.

"My turn now," said the Judge.

> *"In the spring the happy goatlet*
> *Perches on the garden fence,*
> *While the robin with his notelet*
> *Warbles forth a tune immense—"*

"How can the goatlet perch on a garden fence if he's in the spring?" asked the Crocodile. "They don't have fences in springs—at least, not in the springs I've drank out of. Strikes me, that's silly."

"You're mixed," cried the Judge, with a frown. "I mean the season."

"I don't know of any seasons called spring," retorted the Crocodile. "Pepper and salt and vinegar are all the seasons I ever eat."

"Oh, but you're stupid," snapped the Judge.

"I have to be, to keep even with jokes like that," retorted the Crocodile. "Any more?"

"How do you like this?" said the Judge.

"'George,' said George Washington's father, 'didn't your mother tell you to decline a second piece of pie at Mrs Brown's yesterday?'

"'Yes, father,' said George.

"'And yet you disobeyed her,' said Mr Washington.

"'I couldn't help myself, father,' said the future Father of his Country. 'Mrs Brown asked me if I didn't *want* another piece, and I had to say yes, because I *did* want another piece. I couldn't tell a lie.'

"'Come out into the wood-shed, my son,' said Augustine Washington. 'You have worked that joke off on me once too often, and I propose to correct the chestnut with the application of a little birch.' How's that?"

"Don't believe it ever happened," said the Crocodile, wearily, as his tears gushed forth with such renewed vigour that Rollo, to escape a thorough soaking, climbed up on a huge boulder, back of the two jokers. "You'll have me fast asleep, first thing we know."

"Oh, you try him, Mr Punch," said the Judge, impatiently. "He's harder than ever this morning."

"Very well," said Mr Punch. "Here goes. Now, listen to this, Crocky:—

"'That's a rare sight,' said Jones, during the recent coal strike.

"'What is?' asked Smithers.

"'Anthracite,' replied Jones."

The effect of this upon the Crocodile was appalling. If he had been weeping before, he now became a perfect Niagara of tears. They burst forth from his eyes in such overwhelming quantity that, in an instant, what had been a road became a rushing stream of water, which deluged everything, overflowed the embankment, and actually swamped the two jokers sitting thereon.

"Help!" cried Mr Punch, as he was swept from his seat into the torrent.

"Rollo! Rollo! Throw me a rope, or I shall drown," shrieked the Judge. "Quick!" And both the little jokers disappeared beneath the waves.

"Serves you right," growled the Crocodile, plunging in after them, "but I'll save you just the same. Your jokes are awful, but you don't deserve to be drowned for that."

And in a moment Rollo was very much relieved to see his two friends bob up out of the water again, and scramble breathlessly up on the Crocodile's back.

"Great Scott!" groaned the Judge, as he reached a point of safety, "that was a narrow escape."

"It was, indeed," sighed the Crocodile, paddling across, and landing his drenched victims at Rollo's side. "For you, and for me, too. I never had such a narrow escape in my life before."

"You?" snapped Mr, Punch, as he gazed out upon the water at his book of jokes that was floating away down the stream. "Pah! What did you escape from?"

"Laughing," said the Crocodile. "When that wave struck you two humorists, and washed you off the bank, you looked so funny I nearly laughed. If it wasn't for my politeness and the danger of your drowning, I think, for once in my life, I should have cracked a smile."

"It would take a sledge-hammer to crack one of your smiles," sniffed Mr Punch, angrily.

Whereupon the Crocodile began weeping again, and in a moment swam sorrowfully off in his own tears without another word.

Chapter VI

A Visit to the Sphinx

"He may be a Crocodile," said the Judge, as the Crocodile disappeared up the stream, "but, to my mind, he measures up to what you American boys would call a lobster. Just look at my clothes. I don't believe I shall ever be dry again."

Mr Punch laughed. "If you were as dry as that last joke of yours," he said, "you'd be on the edge of spontaneous combustion. As for me, I think we got pretty much what we deserved. We weren't the funniest things alive this time—especially with your poem about the goatlet perched on the garden fence. That kind of poetry is pretty tiresome."

"Well, it's a stand-off with your joke about anthracite," retorted the Judge. "That was a pretty bad pun even for you. If you'd said something about the scarcity of hard coal making it a bit too minus—"

"Bit what?" demanded Mr Punch.

"Bit too minus," said the Judge. "Bit-u-minous—don't you see? Ha, ha! That's not bad. If you'd said something like that, it would have been worthwhile."

"It would have been expensive at a cent a ton," growled Mr Punch. "I'll leave it to Rollo if that isn't the very worst joke he ever heard."

"Oh, please don't," cried Rollo. "I like the jokes of both of you ever so much, and, anyhow, the ones you got off were plenty good enough for a Crocodile, it seems to me."

"Good boy," said Mr Punch. "You'll get along all right, and now what shall we do?"

"I'm going home to hang on the clothes-line until I get dry again," said the Judge. "And then I think I'll go down to the laundry and have myself ironed out. I shall be all wrinkled up to-morrow if I don't. So long. Bye-bye, Rollo."

And the little chap trotted off.

"Well, here we are alone again," said Mr Punch, "as the ten-dollar bill said to the five after their owner had lent them to a friend for the second time. What shall we do—get an axe and crack a few jokes, or would you like to go off to the Sahara and visit the Sphinx?"

"Let's visit the Sphinx," said Rollo, "if we have time."

"We haven't much, but we might get some if old daddy Tempus were about," said Mr Punch. "I wonder if we ca'n't find him somewhere."

Just then there was a scurrying sound up the road, as if in response to the speaker's remark, and Mr Punch jumped up on the upper rail of a near-by fence to see what it was.

"Hooray!" he cried. "We're in great luck, Rollo, my boy. It's old Father Time himself, and he's coming mighty fast, I can tell you; but if you can grab him by the forelock as he passes, and hold him up, we can get all the spare hours we need."

"Kind of like highway robbery, isn't it?" laughed Rollo.

"Exactly; but the old gentleman likes it. Hurry up and get on the embankment, so's you can reach, cried Mr Punch. "Be quick, or you'll miss him."

Rollo scrambled up onto the bank, and, looking up the road whence the scurrying sounds had come, he was pleased to see the old gentleman the Stork had introduced to him coming along at a terrific rate of speed considering his age.

"Clear the road!" he cried. "Look out, for I'm in a fearful hurry. I've got a leap year on my hands shortly, and that extra day keeps me very busy."

"Don't get excited now, Rollo," whispered Mr Punch. "Just grab his forelock as he flies, and we'll get all the time we need."

Father Time was barely ten yards away by this, and coming directly at Rollo. The lad, steadying himself by clutching a small tree at his side with his left hand, reached forward and, as the hurrying figure came close to him, he caught him by the long white lock that grew from his forehead.

"Why, hello, Rollo," said Father Time, as he saw who it was that had caught him. "That you? I thought you'd gone home."

"Not yet," said Rollo, politely, for he was really a little uneasy about his own behaviour. He didn't think it was quite nice or respectful for a little fellow such as he was to treat a white-haired old gentleman with such seeming rudeness. He wouldn't have thought of doing such a thing if he were back in his own home, but here, of course, things were different. "I suppose I ought to go home, Mr Time," he added. "But—"

"Tempus is my real name, Sonny," said the old gentleman.

"Excuse me, Mr Tempus," said Rollo, correcting himself instantly. "I suppose I ought to have gone home long ago, but I've enjoyed myself so much here that I want to stay and see more of Emblemland. Perhaps you can spare me a minute or two."

"Oh, nonsense," said Mr Punch from the other side of the road. "Ask him for a week. We ca'n't do anything with a minute or two."

Father Time smiled benignantly at Mr Punch, and said: "A week is a good deal to ask, Mr Punch."

"That's the reason I told him to ask for it, sir," returned Mr Punch, civilly. "I thought if he asked you for a week, you might at least give him twenty-four hours."

"Oh, I can spare that for Rollo," said Mr Tempus, pleasantly. "In fact, he so seldom wastes any when he has it that I'm inclined to give him forty-eight. Will that be enough?"

"Loads," said Mr Punch. "Make it day-time, will you?"

"Certainly," said Mr Tempus, agreeable as you please. He put his scythe down on the bank alongside of Rollo, and his hour-glass as well, and began fumbling in his cloak as if in search of something. In a moment he had extracted a huge wallet from a pocket way inside the folds of his garment, and, opening it, took out a great bundle of crisp notes that looked for all the world like five-dollar bills.

"These are drafts on the Bank of Time," he said, as he took them out. "Each one is good for one hour—and be careful, my lad, how you spend them."

The kindly old gentleman counted out forty-eight of these notes, and placed them in Rollo's hands.

"And now, since you are a pretty good boy, Rollo, and are generally pretty careful of me, as a special reward, here is an extra quarter for you," and he handed the boy three shining nickel coins, each of which he said entitled the bearer to five minutes. "They may come in handy some time—and now, good-bye."

"Thank you very much, Mr Tempus," said Rollo. "You are very kind. I shall keep these nickels forever."

"Oh, don't do that," said Mr Tempus. "Time is not of any value unless you use it; only see that you use it well. By the way, where are you going?"

"To the Sahara," said Mr Punch.

"Splendid," cried Father Time. "You can do me a good turn there if you will. I'm running a little short of sand for my hour-glasses, and I'd be very much obliged if you'd send me up a couple of cart-loads from the desert."

"I'll surely do it," replied Mr Punch.

"And I'll help load the carts," said Rollo.

"Very kind, I am sure," said Father Time, picking up his scythe and glass, and shaking hands with Rollo. "I must be off. My love to the Sphinx."

With which the old fellow started to run again, and quickly disappeared in the distance.

"I was afraid he'd be angry when I caught hold of his hair," said Rollo.

"Not he!" exclaimed Mr Punch. "There's nothing pleases him more. That's what he keeps his forelock for. And now, Rollo, for the Sphinx."

"How do we get there?" asked the little traveller.

"Well, there's just two ways," Mr Punch replied. "You can either walk around, or you can jump. If you go overland, it's a very long distance; but, if you have the courage to jump into the bottomless pit, you'll come out at the other end, and there's Egypt. The walk will take about a month; the jump, two minutes and a half."

"Let's jump," said Rollo.

"Very well," said Mr Punch. "Come along."

The small couple walked along the road until they came to a huge slab lying across it, along-side of which was a sign bearing the legend:

> SHORT ROUTE TO THE
> SAHARA
> VIA THE LONG JUMP.

In the top of the slab a ring was inserted, upon which Mr Punch began tugging away with all the strength at his command.

"My, but it's heavy!" he groaned, as he pulled and pulled again without any visible result.

"Maybe I can help you," said Rollo. "I'll put my arms about your waist, and we'll both pull together."

"We might do that, or I might go back to the Poetry Mill, and get one of their tender little poems that is pathetic enough to move a heart of stone."

"That would take too long," said Rollo. "If we'd only thought, we might have kept the Crocodile, and got him to weep on the slab. I've heard that the constant flow of water, drop by drop, will wear away the hardest rocks."

"That would never do," said Mr Punch. "That old Crocodile's tears would fill the pit up in a minute, and we couldn't possibly get through without being drowned. I guess, maybe, your idea of a long, strong pull together will do the business."

So Mr Punch and Rollo bent themselves to the work in hand, and, while it was the toughest tug-of-war Rollo had ever taken part in, they were rewarded at last by the complete removal of the stone. It was a dark and forbidding hole that now disclosed itself, and Rollo began to wish he hadn't accepted the invitation to visit the Sphinx. He was not at all ambitious to jump into so dismal a looking place as the bottomless pit appeared to be.

"H–how far is it, Mr Punch?" he stammered, after he had gazed into the opening.

"A trifle over seven thousand miles," said Mr Punch.

"And how about the other end?" demanded Rollo. "What do you land on?"

"Oh, you just come out into the air without landing on anything," Mr Punch explained. "That's the reason it's a harmless jump. If you landed on something at the other end, you might dislocate your eyebrow, or sprain your ankle, or get jarred pretty badly."

"I don't think I quite like it," said Rollo, drawing back.

"Oh, nonsense," said Mr Punch. "Brace up, and be a man. Watch me."

And with this, the little fellow dove into the hole and disappeared way down in its black depths. Not a sound followed his disappearance, and Rollo sat anxiously awaiting the results of his friend's seemingly rash action. For five minutes was he kept in suspense, and then, all of a sudden, Mr Punch popped head first out of the hole again, went up about three feet in the air and, returning, alighted on his feet on the grass along-side of his companion, safe and sound.

"There," he said, "I've been both ways, and without any more effort than falling off a log. You saw how I came out here. That's exactly the way you come out at the other end, only there you alight on the sand instead of on the grass."

"But where does the hole go?" asked Rollo, still a little uneasy over the venture.

"Straight through the earth to the other side," explained Mr Punch. "Come along; don't be such a scaredy-cat."

And Rollo, who had never been able to stand being called a scaredy-cat, cast his fears to the winds and plunged in, head first, diving just as had Mr Punch. His companion followed him immediately. It was, indeed, a very long dive, and the minutes that it took seemed to Rollo like so many months. His first sensation was that of falling, and he was conscious that, as he went along further and further, he was falling faster and faster, and then he began to slow up, as if somebody had put a brake on him. A great white light suddenly appeared ahead of him, and then, in an instant, out he popped into the open again, rose up two or three feet in the air, just as Mr Punch had done at the other end, and, returning, dropped lightly upon the soft sands of a great desert. Hardly had his feet touched the earth when Mr Punch, too, appeared and dropped beside him.

"My!" cried Rollo, breathlessly. "That was great, wasn't it?"

"Nothing like it anywhere," assented Mr Punch. "Chuting the Chutes or Looping the Loop are not to be mentioned in the same day with the long jump. And it's absolutely safe."

"Doesn't anybody ever get caught inside?" asked the boy, as he thought over the possible accidents of such a journey.

"Never yet," said Mr Punch. "The centre of gravity takes care of that. It pulls you down faster and faster every second, and then slows you up after you have passed it, and so keeps you from tumbling off the earth into space after you come out."

"It's wonderful," said Rollo.

"Oh, yes—quite so," agreed Mr Punch. "But not more so than some other things I could tell you if we had time, which we haven't. Stir your stumps, my lad, and let us be moving; it's half a mile to where the Sphinx lives, and we have already spent too large a proportion of your extra hours."

Over the long, dreary stretch of sand Rollo and Mr Punch trod their way, until they came upon a huge sandstone figure rising up from the desert, and gazing fixedly into the far-distant horizon. It was an awesome-looking figure with the crouched body of a huge beast and the strange head of a woman, and what added to the solemnity of the moment was the fact that it never moved its head or its eyes or its mouth, not even when it talked, which it began immediately to do.

"Hello, Punchy!" it said in a kindly tone of voice, which more than made up for its lack of a smile of welcome. "Come after some more jokes for your paper?"

"Not this time, Mrs Sphinx," returned Mr Punch, with a low bow to the strange creature. "I've got all the Egyptian jokes I shall need for several weeks yet. I have come to present you to my friend Rollo."

"Rollo Periwinkle?" demanded the Sphinx, never for a moment taking his eye off the horizon line.

"The very same," said Mr Punch.

"Good!" cried the Sphinx. "I have been wishing he'd come here to see me. I've got some riddles I want to ask him. Sit down, wo'n't you?"

The visitors did as they were bade, taking up their seats on a mound of sand directly in front of the Sphinx's pedestal, and the weird old creature immediately began.

CHAPTER VII

The Sphinx and Others

"You're in great luck, Rollo," Mr Punch whispered as they took their seats in front of the Sphinx. "She doesn't often talk, and even then she contents herself with asking riddles. It's very evident that *you* are going to have an interview."

"I hope she doesn't ask me many questions," said Rollo. "I don't like to answer questions very much. I get enough of that at school."

"I doubt if she does anything else," Mr Punch answered. "But she's got so many to ask, she doesn't really expect any answers—in fact, she's apt to be angry if you do answer her."

"Oh, then I don't care," said Rollo. "Questions are easy if you don't have to answer them."

"I'd like to ask you, Rollo Periwinkle," said the Sphinx, in a voice that rumbled like distant thunder, "a few questions about boys."

"Very well," said Rollo. "I shall be very glad to have you do so."

"Good," returned the Sphinx. "That being the case, here goes:—

> *"Why is it that the little boy,*
> *His father's pride, his mother's joy,*
> *Delights far more in sport that's muddy*
> *Than in the pleasures of the study?"*

"I didn't know that he did," said Rollo. "But then there are others."

> *"Why is it that the tiny lad,*
> *Who ought to make his sister glad,*
> *Delights to tease her so that she*
> *Is full of tears and misery?"*

continued the Sphinx.

"I really couldn't tell you," said Rollo. "You see, I haven't any sister."

> *"Why is it that one piece of pie,*
> *However big and spruce and spry,*
> *Is never by the small boy reckoned*
> *One half so good as is the second?"*

the Sphinx asked.

"Because the second piece is twice as good as the first," said Rollo. "It's as good as the first piece plus its own goodness."

> *"Why is it when the apple's here*
> *About the Autumn of the year*
> *The small boy everywhere is seen*
> *Eschewing ripe and munching green?"*

demanded the Sphinx, with a rumble of displeasure at Rollo's answer.

"Because—" began Rollo.

"Shut up," whispered Mr Punch. "You'll have her very angry if you don't keep quiet."

> *"What is the fun in that queer game—*
> *I think that Football is its name—*
> *That boys delight their coats to doff*
> *And kick each other's noses off?"*

continued the Sphinx.

"We don't," cried Rollo.

"Well, then, I'll put it differently," returned the Sphinx, petulantly.

> *"What is the joy in that strange sport—*
> *Football—to which small boys resort.*
> *In which they very seldom bother*
> *About the ball, but kick each other?*

"I never play the game myself," continued the Sphinx, "so, of course, I don't know."

"Good thing you don't!" exclaimed Rollo. "I'd hate to get into a scrimmage with a person as heavy as you in the game."

"I'd hate it myself," observed the Sphinx, "because I don't see any fun in it. There were a lot of chaps up here the other day playing for dear life, and all they did was to grab each other round the middle, or by the leg, and throw each other down. The safest person in the game seemed to me to be the ball."

"They must have been a couple of scrub elevens," said Rollo, with dignity, for he was himself a great admirer of the game.

"I don't know about that," said the Sphinx. "But I do know that a hard scrubbing would have done them all a lot of good when they got through. How do you like my riddles?"

"They are very interesting," said Rollo.

"Thank you," said the Sphinx, apparently pleased, though she never even cracked a smile. "I'm the great Riddler of the Universe, and the best part of my riddles is that nobody can guess the answers."

"Why is that, Sphinxy?" asked Mr Punch, a question he had asked so many times before that he was afraid the Sphinx would not like it if it were overlooked this time.

"Oh, I imagine it's because generally most often they haven't got any—like those I got off some years ago. 'Why does a Carrot' and 'Why should a Turnip' and 'When was the Cabbage' and 'Who's What'—"

"I don't see much good in a riddle that hasn't got any answer," Rollo put in, forgetting Mr Punch's warning.

"Oh, you don't, eh?" sneered the Sphinx. "Then there's no use of wasting any time over you. What ever induced you to bring such a dull young person to see me, Mr Punch?"

"I didn't mean to be impolite, Mrs Sphinx," said Rollo, before Mr Punch had a chance to answer. "I think your riddles are great—especially 'Who's What' and 'Why does a Carrot'—"

"Then why," asked the Sphinx, "did you say you don't see any use in riddles without answers?"

Rollo scratched his head in perplexity for a minute, and then he answered, "I guess maybe there isn't any answer to that, is there?"

"Ah! Now you are behaving yourself properly," said the Sphinx, more amiably. "That's the way I like to hear you talk, although there really is an answer to that last one. You *didn't* see the good of such riddles, until you heard mine, eh? That it?"

"That's exactly it," said Rollo, with a smile that quite won the old Sphinx's heart, and everything was pleasant again.

"I had a sort of an idea, Mrs Sphinx," Mr Punch remarked, about this point, "that possibly you would be willing to recite some of your poems to Rollo. To my mind they are among the finest poems of the ages and I should like it very much if my young friend here could only hear them."

"Dear me!" cried Rollo, delighted at Mr Punch's suggestion. "Do you write poetry, Mrs Sphinx? I never knew that."

"I rather imagine, young man," returned the Sphinx, "that there is a great deal you don't know yet. You haven't had time to find everything out. I should judge from your appearance that you are a long ways from seventy-five years old yet and I am seventy-five hundred years old. So you'd better be careful about knowing too much in my presence. Of course, I write poetry. Why shouldn't I?"

Rollo couldn't see any reason why not, and said so frankly.

"I don't see how you do it, though," he added.

"Oh, that's easy enough," said the Sphinx, loftily. "I do it every moonlit night after everybody about here has gone to bed. I come down off of my pedestal here and creep over on the Sahara and with the forenail of my right claw I write upon the sands some of the most beautiful verses you ever heard, full of rhyme and mystery. Some of them are short and some of them are long. Some of them have only one line and others are miles long. The biggest one I ever did was called 'Rubber', and it stretched half way across the desert and back again. That's why I called it 'Rubber'—it stretched so far—although it was really about clam-shells."

"What do you do with them?" asked Rollo, much interested. "Sell them to the papers?"

"No, indeed," answered the Sphinx. "I don't do anything with them. I just leave them out there on the sand and the Wind comes along and wafts them away. I don't really know what becomes of them, but I think probably the Wind blows them to market somewhere, for I notice it takes all I write and certainly it wouldn't do that if it weren't for some purpose. Indeed, I learned last week that a poem I wrote over a hundred years ago called '*Humpty Dumpty*' was printed in England over the name of Mrs Goose—or something like that. It ran this way:—

> *"Humpty Dumpty sat on a wall,*
> *Humpty Dumpty had a big fall—"*

"Did you write that?" cried Rollo.

"I did, indeed," said the Sphinx. "Why? Ever hear it before?"

"Well rather," said Rollo. "It's in my Mother Goose book."

"That's it—that's the lady's name," said the Sphinx. "Mother Goose. She's the one. I did that one night—oh, a great many years ago—and the Wind came along and blew it away along with a rhyme called '*Robin and Richard*':—

> *"Robin and Richard were two pretty men*
> *Who lay in bed till the clock struck ten—"*

"Mother Goose got that too," said Rollo.

"No doubt," sighed the Sphinx, "and never gave me no credit neither, I'll warrant you. Then I had another that I never heard from afterward. Let's see—how did it begin? Ah, yes!

> *"'Twas the night before Christmas*
> *when all through the house*
> *Not a creature was stirring,*
> *not even a mouse.*
> *And I in my nightcap—"*

"Why," cried Rollo, "I've got that printed in a book with a whole lot of coloured pictures to it. And I love it."

"Thank you kindly," observed the Sphinx. "I rather liked that myself. The Wind didn't leave that out in the sand five minutes."

"I shouldn't think you'd like it much, having other people get your poetry," said Rollo.

"And why not, pray?" asked the Sphinx. "What's poetry for? You don't write poetry just to put it in a box and bury it, do you?"

"No," said Rollo. "But if you wrote it, I should think you'd like to have people know it."

"Oh, I don't care anything about that," said the Sphinx. "I haven't any use for fame. Fame isn't any good and only makes other people jealous of you. I know I'm smart and that satisfies me. I don't care whether anybody else knows it or not. Some of my poems, however, I like so much I keep them in my head and never write at all. My '*Poems of the Sea*', for instance, I've just composed while I've been sitting up here without any attempt at putting them down, and as long as I have them stowed away in the back of my head, the Wind nor nobody else can get hold of them. I'll tell you some of them if you'd like."

"Delighted," said Rollo.

"Well, the first one was about '*The Jilted Oyster*'," said the Sphinx. "It's very pathetic and may make you cry just a little bit, but it's strong—stronger than a great many things that have become famous. Sit perfectly still, now, so as not to disturb my metre, and I'll recite it to you."

Rollo crossed his hands in his lap and Mr Punch bowed his head, while the Sphinx recited the poem of "*The Jilted Oyster*":—

"The Oyster was a gallant bold
Who loved a Soft Shell Crab.
He called upon her, so I'm told,
Dressed up in pink and drab—
Up to her residence he rolled
In a brand-new hansom cab.

He told her that he deemed her sweet—
A perfect little prize.
He made remarks about her feet,
And also praised her eyes,
And other things I sha'n't repeat,
But all of them likewise.

He offered her his heart and hand
Down on his bended knee,
And other things so great and grand
They would have conquered me—
A handsome house upon the land,
A home beneath the sea.

He told her that he'd stores of gold
*   And chests of precious stone—*
His cellar was completely coaled
*   From mines that he did own,*
But "Oh," he cried, "my life is mould
*   Because I live alone.*

"If you will come and be my bride,"
*   He cried in accents brief,*
"In silks and satins you may ride,
*   Of princesses the chief.*
Great happiness will us betide
*   And squelch my ghoulish grief."*

But she, this haughty crab so fair,
*   The Oyster would not wed.*
She rose out of her rocking-chair
*   And, tossing high her head,*
She sent him from her in despair
*   Back to his oyster-bed:*

Because he was so very meek,
*   Was lacking so in force,*
She couldn't stand him for a week
*   Without tabasco sauce,*
And that made marriage, so to speak,
*   Impossible, of course.*

Poor wight! In gloom he took his way
*   Back through the salty tide*
Made deeper by the tearful spray
*   That bubbled from his side,*
And later on, the gossips say,
*   Committed suicide*

By striding out upon the sand—
So bitter was his cup—
Nigh to a busy oyster-stand
Where people came to sup,
And there upon the wintry strand
Was straightway gobbled up."

"Wasn't that painful?"

"Squeeze out a tear, Rollo," whispered Mr Punch. "Quick, or the Sphinx wo'n't like it."

"D–dreadfully s–sad," sobbed Rollo.

"I thought you'd enjoy that," said the Sphinx, complacently. "That's the kind of gloom that means something. It moved me very strangely, that poem did, and I tried every which way to let the Oyster down easy, but I couldn't. He'd got himself into trouble by falling in love with the Crab in the first place and I had to leave him to his fate. Now with the Eel I had better luck. You can do more with an eel than you can with an oyster anyhow, because there's more give to him. Just listen to this, '*The Talented Eel*':—

"The Eel, the Eel, the wiggly Eel,
How very happy he must feel!
I sometimes truly envy him,
For he is always in the swim,
And when he goes abroad to dine
And seats himself with people fine.
He does not bother with a tie
That comes undone and goes awry,
But twists his graceful figure so
Himself becomes a perfect bow.

"Eh? How'd you like to be able to do that and become your own necktie, Rollo?" added the Sphinx.

"Splendid," cried Rollo, clapping his hands with pleasure.

"I wish I could do it," said the Sphinx, "but then there's no use wishing a thing like that. When you're going to wish you might as well wish for something you have a chance of getting, and never as long as I live can I tie myself into a bow-knot, and I don't believe you can either. Here's another—about '*The Gudgeon*':—

> *"The Gudgeon is a curious bird*
> *Of whom you have already heard.*
> *He doesn't know a single thing*
> *And spends his time a-wondering;*
> *And such a curious mixture too!*
> *You'd almost think it wasn't true,*
> *And yet his mouth, upon my soul,*
> *Looks like a little golfing hole,*
> *He has no nose of any size*
> *And when you look into his eyes*
> *The wise man finds that each compares*
> *With nothing but a flight of stares.*

"That's one of the best descriptive poems I ever wrote," said the Sphinx.

"Ca'n't you almost see the Gudgeon?" exclaimed Mr Punch, nudging Rollo violently. And then he added in a whisper. "Laugh! The Sphinx means you to laugh at that."

Rollo did as lie was bade, and the Sphinx to reward him gave him one more rhyme and then wished him good-night.

"I'll give you just one more, Rollo," she said. "It is called '*The Fortunate Lobster*':—

> "*The lobster is a lucky fish,*
> *As well as a most toothsome dish,*
> *For when he's in the soup, you see,*
> *Instead of finding misery*
> *He's just as happy as can be.*
> *A man who's in the soup you'll find*
> *Is always troubled in his mind.*
> *Just why this is is very plain:*
> *One creature's joy's another's pain.*
> *Some folk were made to sing and dance,*
> *And some were made to sew on pants,*
> *And some were made to preach or write,*

And some were made to toil and fight,
And some were made to loop-the-loop—
But Lobsters, they were made for soup.
And so when in the soup he gets
The Lobster has no sad regrets.
He's done the thing he came to do—
I truly wish the same for you.

"Good and very moral, don't you think?"

"I do, indeed, Mrs Sphinx, and I thank you very much for a pleasant hour," said Rollo.

"You are very welcome," said the Sphinx, graciously. "And now good-bye. Come again some time, and I'll tell you some of my jokes—which I haven't time to do now, for the Sandman is due and I must get his load ready for him."

And Rollo bidding the Sphinx good-night, walked along on his way with Mr Punch.

"What did she mean by the Sandman?" asked Rollo, as they trudged along the desert.

CHAPTER VIII

Rollo Meets Some International Emblems

"What?" cried Mr Punch, with a great show of surprise at Rollo's question. "Don't you know who the Sandman is? Well, I am astonished. I thought every small boy in creation knew the Sandman. Why, he's the Emblem of Sleepiness."

"Oh—that one," said Rollo. "Of course, I knew all about him. I never knew there was any such person really though. I don't think I ever even saw his picture."

"And for a very good reason," returned Mr Punch. "He's one of the few Emblems who've never had their pictures taken. Fact is, he couldn't have his picture taken because he's invisible. He might sit all day in front of a Kodak and it wouldn't do any good at all. I don't believe he ever saw himself."

"No, I never did," came a melancholy voice directly in front of the little travellers. "And I've tried lots of times. I've stood for hours right before a looking-glass and never a once did I catch a glimpse of me."

Rollo jumped backward, a little startled to hear a voice that apparently came out of nothing at all. It was just a bit too mysterious to be pleasant.

"Wh–what was that?" he asked, clutching Mr Punch nervously by the arm.

"Don't be afraid, Rollo," said the voice, in a kindly tone, which made the boy feel easier in his mind. "It's only me, and I wouldn't hurt you for all the world."

It's the Sandman himself," said Mr Punch. "And a very nice useful chap he is. Rollo, Sandman. Sandman, Rollo."

"Oh, we've met before," came the invisible voice. "At least I have, lots and lots of times. I deliver sand at Rollo's house pretty nearly every night, and in large quantities too. If it wasn't for me, I doubt if Rollo, or his brother Teddy, or his friend Neddy Tomlinson would ever want to go to bed."

Here the Sandman laughed heartily.

"They'd be regular Owls if it wasn't for me," he added. "And so would most other children."

"Owls?"asked Rollo.

"Yep!" said the Sandman. "Owls. You'd stay up all night and sleep all day if you could, just as Owls do, but I fix that up by coming around and chucking sand in your eyes.

"I am the man that brings the sand
To children on the sea and land
At eve when twilight hours creep
Across the mountain, and the deep,
And bring their tired eyelids sleep,

I am the fellow strange and odd
Who guides you to the land of Nod;
Who takes you to the Vale of Dreams
Where nothing's quite the thing it seems,
And empty plans are wondrous schemes.

I am the chap who comes by night
When gas-jets all are burning bright,
And, spite of every if and but,
And pooh and bah, and tush and tut,
Sits on your lids and keeps 'em shut.

I am the friend of little boys,
And little girls and little toys,
Who, as the sun sinks in the west,
Comes riding forth to be the guest
Of those who must be wooed to rest

The friend of every sleepyhead
Who doesn't want to go to bed;
The comrade of the little chap
Who doesn't like his sleeping-cap,
Yet really ought to take his nap.

No harm to anyone do I,
But good to all is what I try;
And those who toil for Love or Fame,
Who work, or play, 'tis all the same.
The young and old all bless my name.

Of all the blessings on the list
There's none like Dreamland's tender tryst
And on the land and on the deep,
On fertile plain and desert sweep,
There's none so sweet and true as sleep."

"Every word of that is true, Rollo," said Mr Punch, "and you owe this great blessing to the dear old Sandman. Some time when he comes around and you aren't quite ready for him, you must remember that he comes only for your good;

that if he stayed away from you for more than a day, or were to be neglectful of you for any reason, you would miss him more almost than anything else in the whole world. He brings you rest, and health, and happy dreams. He carries you through the dark and gloomy hours of the night, watching over you tenderly and faithfully, and then when the bright hours of the morning come, he goes on his way to prepare for his next visit, to fill up his basket with sand and to do everything he can to make you a good, strong, healthy man."

"I like him very much indeed," said Rollo, a little shame-facedly as he thought of the many hard fights he had put up against the gentle ministrations of this kindly friend. "Next time he comes to my house, I'll behave better—"

"Oh, that's all right," said the Sandman, with a laugh. "Just because I'm me, don't you stop being you, my dear Rollo. I don't mind having a tussle getting you off to bed any more than you mind a good stiff game of football with a lot of other fellows of your own size. Indeed, as long as I know I am going to win in the end, I rather enjoy it."

"I wish I could see you," said Rollo.

"I wish you could," replied the Sandman, with a wistful note in his voice. "I wish I could see myself, but it may not be. My work requires that I shall be invisible—I couldn't get where I could throw my sand if people could see me coming—and I must be satisfied. It's good work and I ought not to complain because I don't appear to be anybody at all. How do you go back to Emblemland?"

"The Jump," said Mr Punch. "It's the shortest way."

"Well, so long," said the Sandman. "I've got to get busy. There are about eight million boys over in the United States that have been to the circus lately and it's the hardest thing in the world to get them to go to sleep. They go to bed all right, but they don't want to close their eyes for a minute with their circus games. I had to use five quarts of sand on just one boy last night who was making a huge circus tent out of the bed-clothes, and even then he flopped around all night long. Bye-bye, Rollo. I'll be around at your house about nine o'clock to-night."

And the voice, humming a happy little tune, faded away in the distance.

"Good old chap!" cried Mr Punch, as the Sandman made off. "I don't know what the world would do without him."

"His business must use up a fearful lot of sand," said Rollo.

"It does," said Mr Punch, "but there's plenty of it here. Fact is, that's all the Sahara is good for. And now come along. Let's leave our order for Father Time's supply and get back to Emblemland as quickly as we can."

A call was made at the Delivery Office, which to Rollo was very like one of the pyramids, pictures of which were to be found in his geography, where twenty cartloads of the finest hour-glass sand were ordered sent to Mr Tempus, and then the little fellows once more dove down into the bottomless pit, and five minutes later were sitting under the trees of Emblem-land none the worse for their adventure. While the returned travellers were talking over the experiences of the trip to the land of the Sphinx, Rollo was somewhat disturbed to hear a fearful roaring in the woods back of him.

"Mercy me, Mr Punch!" he cried. "That sounds like a wild beast."

"Sounds so, but it isn't," replied Mr Punch. "It's only my good old friend the British Lion. He's the greatest ever, and I think cares more for my jokes than anybody else in the world. He's like the little girl with the curl, that old Lion is. When he's good, he's very, very good, but when he's bad—oh, he's terrific. Here he comes. I'll introduce you to him."

Glancing down the road, Rollo saw a strange sight, and yet in view of all that had already happened to him in this queer country, the lad found nothing very surprising in it. It was, briefly, a huge, masterful-looking Lion, clad in a swallow-tail coat, with a waistcoat resembling the British flag, buckskin breeches, and boots. In his eye he wore a single eye-glass and was walking along as jauntily as if he owned the earth—which I suspect he really thinks he does. As soon as this curious creature caught sight of Mr Punch, he burst into roars of laughter, which echoed and re-echoed through the forest.

"Why, Punchy, old man," he cried, "how do you do?"

"Oh, I'm all write, as the man said who made his living by the pen," replied Mr Punch.

"Magnificent!" roared the Lion, slapping his knee violently with joy at Mr Punch's joke. "And what is this you have with you—a boy?"

"Oh, no," said Mr Punch. "He isn't a boy—he's a hard-boiled egg out on his travels."

Splendid," roared the Lion. "You know how to give the funny answer to the unnecessary question. What's the boiled egg's name?"

"Rollo," said Mr Punch. "Strange name for a hard-boiled egg, but it's the best he's got with him, so it will have to do."

"How-d'ye-do, Rollo," said the Lion, holding out his right paw, which Rollo took somewhat timidly. "Are you English, or what?"

"I'm American," said Rollo.

"A Merican, eh?" said the Lion. "Hum. Let me see—just what is a Merican?"

"I'm an American," Rollo said, correcting himself.

"Oh!" said the Lion. "Well—that's good enough for me. I like Americans and I hope we'll always be good friends, particularly when I have a fight on my hands. Fact is, I've got some American eggs in my own basket and some day perhaps if my food-supply runs short, I'll find them useful. You speak very good English for a boiled egg, Rollo. Fact, I never heard a boiled egg express himself more perfectly, and I beg to assure you that you will always be welcome in my house."

"I hope you have quite recovered from your fight with the Unicorn, Mr Lion," said Rollo, politely.

"Oh, that was easy," laughed the Lion. "He wasn't a good fighter. He had nothing but a horn to fight with, and he hadn't even learned how to blow on that when we met. He'd have made a very good band-leader in time, but as the representative of the British Crown—"

"He'd have looked like thirty cents," said Mr Punch.

"How much is that in English money?" asked the Lion.

"About a quarter of a crown," said Mr Punch, with a grin.

The Lion threw himself down upon the grass and roared with mirth at Mr Punch's joke, although Rollo thought it rather flat, and then rising to his feet, shook hands with Rollo again and made off, his sides still shaking with laughter.

The Lion had barely disappeared at the first turn of the road when the air above them was rent with a terrific screeching, and before the little couple had even the time to look up, a huge American Eagle swooped down before them, and extended his right wing to Rollo with the remark— "Ah! I've found you at last, my boy. There's a great hullabaloo about you at home, sir. You went off without leaving word with anybody as to where you were going. Result is everybody's searching for you. The Navy is scouring the seas, the Army is searching the land. I've got a dozen Eaglets scurrying through the sky after you, and way down in the depths of the Earth the Elves and the Gnomes are seeking traces of you. It's a relief to find you, for we don't want any of Uncle Sam's citizens going about unprotected anywhere. Why didn't you leave word?"

"I—I didn't know I was coming," said Rollo, timidly.

"Well, it's all right, now that I've found you—though really, you're safe enough here in Emblemland," said the Eagle. "What I was afraid of was that perhaps you had gone off to discover the North Pole, or that old Pegasus had run away with you to the Milky Way or something like that.

> *"If you're in reach upon the Earth*
> *You needn't have a doubt*
> *That if you get in trouble*
> *Uncle Sam will help you out.*
>
> *It doesn't matter where you are*
> *South of the Polar Sea,*
> *Or North of the Antarctic,*
> *You can always count on me.*
>
> *But if you're tumbled into space*
> *And landed 'mongst the stars,*
> *On Saturn, Venus, Jupiter,*
> *The Dipper or on Mars,*
>
> *Until we get a Navy built*
> *Of airships stanch and true,*
> *We'd have a mighty awkward time*
> *A-rescuing of you."*

"That'll be a great day, Mr Eagle," put in Mr Punch, "when we Earth people have our airships and go off exploring the Universe."

"Maybe," returned the Eagle, with a doubtful shake of his head. "But I don't know for sure that we'll be any better off. I'd like to know more about the other planets, but I'm not so certain that I'd care to have immigrants crowding into my bailiwick from Saturn, Mars, and the various other regions of the heavens. We've got all we can do swallowing up the Hungarians and the Italians and Poles who swarm in upon us without drawing upon the Solar system for new citizens. I don't mind having Englishmen and Germans come to settle down in my family, but until I know more about them I should draw the line at Saturnians and Martians and Dipperinos. Can you write, Rollo?"

"Certainly I can," returned Rollo.

"Know all the capitals of the Alphabet as well as of Europe?"

"Yes, indeed," said Rollo. "Why?"

"Oh, nothing except that the Russian Bear and I are thinking of getting up an International Circus and we want somebody to write out the programme for us. Do you think you could do it?"

"I could try," said Rollo.

"Very well, then," observed the Eagle, putting his wing around Rollo's shoulder. "Come along. We'll go down to the Ink Well and meet Mr Bear. He's waiting."

Saying good-bye to Mr Punch, who was now due back at the Joke Mill, and thanking him for his kindly service, Rollo went off with the Eagle, and in a short while came to the Ink Well, within the rubbled circular wall of which stood the Russian Bear, awaiting them.

"Mr Bear, this is my young fellow-citizen, Rollo Periwinkle," said the Eagle. "He has kindly consented to act as Secretary for our International Circus."

"Glad to meet you," said the Bear, gruffly. "I've just hauled up a bucketful of ink, and pulled a few quills out of the

Austrian Eagle's tail for you to write with. Seems to me you're pretty young, though, to know how to write."

"We teach 'em young in our country, Mr Bear," said the Eagle. "We don't wait until a man's ninety to let him be educated, the way you do."

"Well, I suppose it's a good plan," said the Bear, "but I don't believe in it myself. It isn't respectful for children to know more than their elders, and in my mind, the youngsters ought to sit back until the old have been waited upon. We ca'n't educate our youngsters until we have provided instruction for their grandparents. Still, you are bringing up Eaglets and I am bringing up Cubs, and what's good for one wo'n't do for the other. So I guess it's all right. Shall we begin?"

"I'm ready," said Rollo, whereupon he threw himself down upon his stomach and, taking the quill the Bear had handed him, began to write out the programme.

CHAPTER IX

The Emblemland Circus

"What'll we call the Circus, anyhow?" asked the Bear as Rollo made ready to write.

"Oh—the International Hagenbeck Show would be pretty good," said the Eagle.

"How would 'The Greatest Show in Space' do?" suggested the Bear, not seeming to care very much for the Eagle's idea.

"'Twouldn't," replied the Eagle. "We don't really know that it is. They may have something vastly finer out in Saturn—fact, I think very likely they have. Why should the planet be provided with a ring and a whole lot of extra suns to light it up with if they hadn't?"

"That isn't a circus ring, is it?" queried the Bear.

"I don't know," said the Eagle. "I never got that far from home, and nobody's told me anything about it. All I do know is that it isn't a finger-ring.

"We might call it 'The Greatest Show in Emblemland'," said the Bear.

"That wouldn't be right, either, because there aren't any others," objected the Eagle.

"Don't let's call it anything then just yet," said the Bear. "Just write out the Programme and maybe the name will come to us later."

"Maybe there wo'n't be any circus at all," said the Eagle, "so I guess we may save time by not naming it. The first thing to do is to get our circus and name it afterward. Now let's see—Rollo, put down the British Lion for an act."

Rollo wrote down the name and waited.

"The British Lion is not good for much," growled the Bear. "What can he do that's funny and likely to amuse the children? He couldn't crack a joke with his back teeth."

"He can roar pretty loud," said the Eagle.

"That wouldn't amuse the children. It would frighten them," growled the Bear, who evidently did not care to have the Lion in the Circus at all. "And you know as well as I do that once he got started, he'd never stop. He wants to be the whole show every time."

"We might let him be the Announcer," said the Eagle. "He could roar out the programme very well indeed. He's got just the voice for it."

"All right," said the Bear. "Put him down for that. And now how about the German Boar? I don't think we'd better let him in the ring, do you? He isn't good for much, and he's always looking for trouble."

"He ca'n't dance," replied the Eagle, "and he ca'n't sing— I don't know what he could do if we did let him in. He might be the Happy Family."

"What—all by himself?" demanded the Bear.

"Yes," said the Eagle. "That's the only way he could be it. He wouldn't be happy if there were anybody else."

"One animal don't make a family, though," said the Bear, shaking his head doubtfully.

"That's true," said the Eagle. "I never thought of that. Perhaps we'd better make him the policeman who keeps order? But that leaves only you and me for the circus part, and as I'm going to take the tickets at the door, of course, I wouldn't be on the programme at all. Getting to be a rather slim show with only you left, I think."

"Oh, I don't know," observed the Bear, drawing himself up proudly. "I'm a pretty good-looking animal. I think I'd make a rather fine spectacle, myself."

"No doubt; but you wouldn't pay to see yourself, would you?" asked the Eagle.

"No—of course I wouldn't," retorted the Bear. "Why should I?"

"I don't know," replied the Eagle. "Nor why anybody else should either. You ca'n't ask people to pay to see something you wouldn't pay to see yourself."

The Bear scratched his head thoughtfully for a moment.

"I never thought of it that way," he said. "You see, I see myself so often that I'm rather tired of myself, and naturally wouldn't think of paying to see myself again."

"Then you'd better not risk it at all," said the Eagle, firmly. "If you're tired of yourself, other people might get tired of you, too, and that would be extremely unpleasant."

The Bear looked sadly down the road.

"I'm tremendously disappointed," he said. "It's always been my ambition to get a position in a circus, and it seemed to me that we could work it so that I could give up my present occupation, which is distasteful to me. I'm awfully tired of being an Emblem in a country like Russia. It's too big, and I have to travel through Siberia and a whole lot of other beastly cold places day in and day out, and without a salary. It's all right for you, who can fly, and are not bothered by bad roads to be the Emblem of a great big country, but I have to walk all the time, and I tell you, Mr Eagle, it is fearfully hard at times."

"Well, I don't see what we can do," said the Eagle. "We ca'n't make an International Circus out of a Russian Bear, so we'd better give it up. If you want me to, I'll make a little side-show of you for my Political Circus. We'd make a lot of money showing 'The Russian Bear in Captivity'—"

"Hoity toity!" retorted the Bear. "Captivity indeed. I'd look well in captivity, wouldn't I?"

"You'd look pleasanter," said the Eagle, dryly.

"What is your Political Circus?" demanded the Bear.

"It consists of three beautiful animals," returned the Eagle. "An Elephant and a Tiger and the cunningest little trained Donkey you ever saw. The Elephant is known all over the land as G.O.P. The Tiger answers to the old Indian name of Tammany, and the Donkey hasn't any name at all, but he's full of awfully funny little tricks."

"I don't think," said the Bear, gruffly, "that I'd like the company. I can stand associating with an Elephant or a Tiger, but I draw the line at Donkeys."

"Very well, old Romanov," returned the Eagle.

"I've done the best I could for you. You've ruled everybody but yourself out of the International Circus, and I don't think that's quite fair. We've been good friends always, but I'm not going to turn my back on all my other friends just for that But any time you want a job as a side-show of mine, all right. Just let me know and I'll be glad to take you in. Until then, good-bye."

The Eagle bowed low to the Bear, who merely showed his teeth in return, and taking Rollo by the hand, made off into the wood with him.

"He's getting mighty lonesome these days, that old Bear," observed the Eagle. "I shouldn't be a bit surprised if he left us altogether and went into partnership with the Chinese Dragon. He's been making up to old Wun Tu Thri for some time past—and if he does—well, old Wun Tu Thri will be gobbled up in less than no time, for Mr Bear is a very crafty old person."

Rollo remembered these words of the Eagle's for a long time after he had tome out of Emblemland, and he has noticed since that his feathered companion was far from wrong in his estimate of the Russian Bear's character. His smile is a very charming one but—it doesn't mean very much, but then no bear's smile ever did. It is no more a sign of a genial disposition than his hug is an evidence of his affection.

"We'll stop in now and see a rehearsal of my Political Show," said the Eagle. "It's really worthwhile."

As the Eagle spoke, they came to a clearing in the road, and not far away from where they stood, lying against a tree, Rollo saw a most beautiful Tiger, scratching its soft fur on the tree-bark and purring like "a ten horse-power kitten", as Rollo put it in describing the incident later.

"My! Isn't she a beauty!" cried Rollo.

"Mmm—yes—to look at," said the Eagle. "But you want to be careful about how you treat her. She wouldn't eat you, but she's very fond of sweets, and if you give her half a chance she'll go through your pockets after 'em quicker than a wink."

"Well, what harm does that do?" said Rollo, walking up to the Tiger's side and stroking the huge creature gently on the head. "Friend of mine home has a pony that does that and everybody thinks it's very nice."

"It's different with the Tiger," replied the Eagle. "Very different. If she'd stick to sugar and candy, it wouldn't be so bad, but she doesn't. If she doesn't find anything of that sort in your pockets, she gobbles up whatever else you may happen to have in 'em: gold watches, jack-knives, diamond rings, and fifty-cent pieces. One day last year she swallowed a big wallet containing a hundred and fifty thousand one dollar bills that a visitor happened to have with him. Another time she made off with a whole lot of diamonds that belonged to Uncle Sam and he's never been able to get any satisfaction out of her at all."

"What a wicked Tiger!" cried Rollo, starting back in fear lest the huge catlike creature should pilfer some of his belongings.

"Well—some people say she isn't wicked, but just doesn't know any better," said the Eagle. "And when she smiles you want to be very careful and not fall in."

"I guess I'll keep away from her altogether," said Rollo.

"That's the wisest course," observed the Eagle. "Dangerous company is always a good thing to avoid. Indeed, it's the only good thing about it."

Just then a great gong sounded, and the Tiger, a moment before the perfect picture of calm beauty, sprang to her feet with a roar that echoed and reechoed throughout the forest, gnashed her teeth and snarled in a truly terrifying manner, and became instead a picture of rage.

"Wh–what's the meaning of all this?" said Rollo, shrinking away from the Tiger and seeking refuge behind the Eagle's protecting wing.

"That's the summons," explained the Eagle. "Every day the Tiger and the Elephant have a boxing contest as a sort of rehearsal for the big fight in which our Political Circus consists. We have an exhibition every four years and these daily fights keep them in practice. The Tiger has been getting the worst of it lately and it makes her mad. Come along and I'll show you a battle royal."

Following the Tiger up the road, Rollo and the Eagle shortly came upon a large field that was concealed from the public eye by a high fence. With a nod at the gate-keeper, the Eagle walked in and the lad followed closely upon his heels. It was a very plain sort of enclosure with no seats at all, and in the centre of it, standing on the grass, facing each other prepared to give battle, were the Tiger and the Elephant. They were a curious-looking pair, and apparently well matched, although the Elephant seemed to have a very decided advantage. The Tiger's forepaws were done up in boxing gloves, which he handled in true scientific fashion, but the Elephant so overmatched him in weight, and wielded the glove upon the end of his trunk so rapidly and vigorously that the poor Tiger seemed to have only half a chance. But as the fight proceeded it became clear that the Tiger's lightness of foot very nearly evened matters up, and when, every now and then, the Donkey with two boxing gloves on his hind hoofs ran into the midst of the fight and kicked the Elephant on the shins, Rollo saw that the contest was not to be so easily won by the Elephant.

It was spirited while it lasted, and Rollo and the Eagle found it wise to climb up upon the fence to keep out of the way, for the two boxers covered very nearly the whole field in their fierce combat. At the end of twenty minutes both contestants were pretty much out of breath, seeing which the tricky little Donkey rushed out to help the Tiger, but before he could quite accomplish his purpose, the Elephant with a well-directed swing of his trunk caught him squarely on the top of his head and bowled him completely over. It was so sudden and unexpected that the Tiger, who was preparing to deliver a  blow that should send the Elephant down to defeat, tripped on her own tail and staggered unsteadily for an instant, and being caught off her guard by the Elephant, was knocked over flat on her back.

"Well, what do you think of that, Rollo?" asked the Eagle, as they climbed down off the fence and prepared to move along.

"It was a pretty good fight," said Rollo. "I think the Tiger might have won if it hadn't been for the Donkey's tricks."

"I sometimes think so myself," said the Eagle, "but we've got to have him. In the first place, the Tiger insists upon it, and in the second, there's no fun in a circus without a clown."

The Tiger and the Donkey, removing their gloves, walked out of the enclosure together, and the Elephant, after the boxing glove had been removed from his trunk, stood meekly at one side until Uncle Sam, who had been an interested spectator of the contest, climbed upon his back.

"He's won again," he said, as he mounted to his seat back of the Elephant's ears. "And now, who wants to take a ride with me on his back?"

"I do," cried Rollo.

"All right," said Uncle Sam. "Scramble up and I'll take you for a visit to my good old friend, Santa Claus. And first, in order that you may be welcome to the old fellow, I will take you to the Hall of Good Intentions and provide you with the necessary credentials."

"What's credentials?" asked Rollo.

"Recommendations," said Uncle Sam. "You wo'n't be welcome to Santa Claus unless you are a tolerably good boy. He doesn't expect you to be a perfect Saint, but he wants to know that you mean well."

And so, clambering to a seat behind Uncle Sam's back, Rollo was transported through the wood to the Hall of Good Intentions.

CHAPTER X

The Hall
of Good Intentions
and Santa Claus

*I*t was a strange place, that Hall of Good Intentions, and was presided over by an old lady who looked so much like Mr Punch that Rollo at first thought it was he dressed up in a nurse's clothes. But it turned out not to be so, but the kindly old wife of Father Time. Rollo didn't know Father Time was married any more than I did until he told me, but it was very pleasant for him to find that such a dear old creature as Mrs Time turned out to be was the best beloved of the fine old gentleman he had met before.

Mrs Time met Rollo at the door of the tremendous hallway, and was soon made acquainted with the lad's name by Uncle Sam.

"He wants to visit Santa Claus, Mrs Time," said the latter, "and I've brought him here to see if he can get a few Good Intentions to recommend him to the old fellow."

"I'll do all I can for him," said Mrs Time. "I'll look up his future and see if I can recommend him.

"My future?" asked Rollo, in some surprise.

"Yes," said Mrs Time. "We ca'n't tell how good your Good Intentions are without seeing what they are coming to, and we've got a record therefore of all that you are going to do and be in the years ahead of us. Of course, the years behind you tell a good deal, but those yet to come are the true test of the value of your Good Intentions. You see that row of books on the left-hand side of the Hall?"

"Yes," said Rollo, glancing down the long line of huge volumes that ran as far as the eye could reach.

"Those are the records of the future," she said. "And all those small babies that you see in the incubators on the other side are the New Years that are to come. Every twelve months we send out a fresh one, and the book which represents the Record for that one is then removed to the Library of the Past. In this way, we keep a careful eye on everything that has been and upon everything that is to be as well."

Rollo was tremendously entertained. "I'd like to see what I'm going to be along about 1925," he said. "Have you got that down?"

"Undoubtedly," said the old lady, "but all this information we keep here is confidential. I couldn't tell you what's going to happen to you even if I wanted to, for it wouldn't be good for you to know. You'd worry over the troublesome things, and be so sure of the big things you are going to do that you wouldn't half try.

"'Tis well to know about the past,
 About the present too,
But what the future holds in store
 And what we're going to do,
'Tis better far the way it is
 To have them hid from view.

You do not worry o'er the woes
 So very sure to be;
And all the interesting sights
 That some day you will see
Would lose most of their interest if
 You saw them now with me.

And if you knew what was to come
 In any future year,
The worries and the joys as well,
 The laughter and the tear,
There'd be no sweet surprise to fill
 Your heart with gladsome cheer.

The worries, they would worry;
 And the jokes would soon be old;

The stories that the future tells
To you would all be told,
And with no new thing in your life
You'd find it drear and cold.

So Nature wise hath wisely ruled
The future sha'n't be shown
Not to the pauper on the street,
Nor King upon his throne,
From frozen fields of North and South
Unto the torrid zone.

"You wouldn't have anything to look forward to, Rollo," the old lady added, as she finished her rhyme, "if I showed you what these books contain, and that would take half the pleasure out of your life. And now, while I am looking up your future, just take a little luncheon. I'll be back soon."

Rollo was inclined to be a trifle indignant at the luncheon, as indeed would most other boys, for it was served like baby-food in a bottle, and he thought he had outgrown that sort of thing, but he was wise enough not to show his real feelings in the matter, and in fact, after he had tasted the contents of the bottle which was labelled "Good Intentions", he found it a very sweet luncheon indeed.

True to her word, Mrs Time returned shortly, her face beaming with pleasure.

"You are all right, Rollo," she said. "I've looked you up as far as your record is written, and I can recommend you to Santa Claus as a young person whose Good Intentions are sterling. I've written a line to him saying so, as follows:

"'Rollo Periwinkle, the Bearer, is a young man with an excellent future. In 1909 he will 9—7—14—26, but by force of hard work he will overcome that and become an 11—97—2—47. His chief work in life, which he will begin in X.Y.Z., will be in the line of 39—46—53, and his success will be between 14 and 37. I confidently recommend him to your kind consideration.'"

"Thank you very much," said Rollo, taking the note the old lady had written and gazing curiously at it. It told him so little about himself beyond the comforting fact that Mrs Time approved of him. "Er—what do those figures mean?"

"Ah!" laughed Mrs Time. "That's telling. They signify certain things that you mustn't know yet, but Santa Claus will understand them, and will receive you accordingly. I'll ring up a reindeer and send you along. I'd keep you here longer, but little 1903 over there is going out into the world very shortly, and I've got to get him dressed."

Suiting her action to her word, Mrs Time touched an electric button, and in less than a jiffy a graceful and gentle reindeer appeared at the doorway prepared to transport the little visitor to the abode of Santa Claus.

"Good-bye, young man," said the kindly old lady, as Rollo mounted the reindeer. "It has been a pleasure to meet you, and any time you happen along this way again don't fail to call on me. A youngster who is going to be a 5—7—11—4—3 at twenty-one, and 4—12—13—75 of the United States at forty is worth knowing."

"I wish I knew what the figures meant," said Rollo.

"Well, I'm glad you don't," laughed Mrs Time. "If you did, they mightn't happen. You'd be too sure, you know, and that would spoil everything."

In a moment, in response to a clucking sound from Mrs Time's lips, the reindeer made a great bound forward, and before Rollo had time even to wave his hand in farewell to his pleasant hostess, they landed in the midst of a brilliant snow-clad scene, with lovely Christmas-trees growing on every hand, sprouting forth toys of the most delicious sort, cornucopias bulging with candies, and sparkling in the glistening light of millions of candles.

And not two hundred yards distant there rose from earth a magnificent structure that shone as if it were built of silver and ice. There were huge towers that at a distance appeared like glorious icicles reaching up into the heavens, and from them flamed the constant yellow glow of a golden illumination. Rollo knew on the instant precisely what this grand building was and what the sprouting Christmas-tree meant, for they could signify only one thing, and that was that he had reached the land of Santa Claus, the dear patron Saint of the Yule-tide, the friend of all little boys and girls, and the guardian of the sweet spirit of Peace and Good-will which has done so much for all mankind in all the many ages past since He who first preached it came to us with His beautiful message.

Treading softly down the avenue through the opening in the Christmas-trees, the Reindeer deposited Rollo on the front door-step of Castle Kris Kringle. Rollo was simply stunned with the beauty of all about him. The air was crisp and cold, but the boy had no feeling but one of genial warmth, because of the spirit of the place which was such as to warm even the tips of his ears, which ordinarily would have stung just a little in the nipping air. Moreover, his ears could not have observed the cold even if they had wished to do so, for they were too busily occupied in drinking in the sweet songs, the beautiful music that welled up from all quarters, blending into one magnificent harmony of sound. He did not notice either that as he mounted the door-step of the Castle, a silvery bell within began to tinkle, as if announcing his coming. Such was the fact, however, and it brought an immediate response and from no less a person than Santa Claus himself.

"Hello, out there," he said, as he opened the door on a crack. "Who's that?"

"It's me—Rollo Periwinkle," replied the little visitor.

"Oh, indeed!" cried Santa Claus, throwing the door wide open and catching Rollo up in his arms. "Glad to see you!

Mrs Time has just telephoned me that you are a 4—7—11—
16—42, and if that's so, you are most welcome. Are you?"

"I don't know what 4—7—11—16—42 means," said Rollo.
"But if Mrs Time told you I was that, I guess I must be, for
she looked up my future."

"Good," said Santa Claus. "You know a thing or two. What
Mrs Time tells you, you can most generally count on as being
correct. Now, come right into my sanctum. You are just in
time for the review and inspection. I've summoned all the toys
for this coming Christmas to a grand parade, just to see if
they're all right. You can sit on my knee and watch them go
by, if you wish to."

It is needless to say that Rollo *did* wish to, and as a result
four minutes later he found himself in the beautiful shop of
Santa Claus, with some five or six hundred thousand lovely
toys passing in parade before him. There were countless

regiments of tin soldiers with brass bands and scouting parties before and behind them; there were wild and tame animals of all sorts and descriptions; great wagon-loads of automatic toys of wondrous variety; marbles, agates, and china alleys until the eye grew bewildered with them; dolls for little girls, dolls that talked, walked and "squalked", as Santa Claus' head carpenter remarked, and every other kind of plaything that you could possibly imagine.

"You see. Master Rollo," said Santa Claus, as the procession passed by, "we've been very busy here this past year. There are millions more children in the world than there used to be, and it's no easy task keeping up with their wishes. My letters for October alone called for 9,000 more Noah's Arks than we've ever put out before. I couldn't tell you how many thousand Ping-Pong sets we've made, and—well, what is it, Jimmie?"

The interruption was caused by the entrance of a carpenter, who had a small toy in his hand.

"Sure, an' it's this Jack Horner, sor," the carpenter said. "We ca'n't keep him supplied wit' plums—"

"What seems to be the matter?" asked Santa Claus.

"He's too human, dis toy, sor," returned the carpenter. "Oi fill the poi up wit' plums an' he shticks in his tumb an' pulls dem out an' ates dem."

Santa Claus laughed heartily.

"Well," he said, "I fancy you'd better make them without

the plums in the pie, Jimmie. We'll send the plums in a box separately and let the youngsters deal them out to him when they feel like it."

"Thankee, sor," said the carpenter. "Anny more orders for de day, sor?" he added.

"Yes, Jimmie. You and Mike bring in the Jack-in-the-Boxes and let Rollo hear them sing."

The order was obeyed instantly, and in a few moments the lad was listening to the most singular music you ever heard. One Jack was singing *"Yankee Doodle"* and *"Dixie"*, and another was splitting his lungs with *"Annie Laurie"*. A third was warbling *"Die Wacht am Rhein"*, while his neighbour was croaking forth *"The Wearing of the Green"* in a cracked voice that if listened to alone would have set the hearer's teeth on edge. Others were trying their voices on the *"Marseillaise"* and *"God Save the King"*, and other national songs from all parts of the world. At first it was a very discordant sound that they were all making, but slowly the notes that did not quite hit it off together seemed to merge themselves into harmony with the strains of *"Yankee Doodle"* and *"Dixie"*, and at the end of two minutes Rollo was astonished at the beauty of the grand combination.

"That's my International Christmas Song," said Santa Claus. "It's a little hard to get used to it at first, but when their voices begin to blend and they get the swing of it altogether, it becomes a Symphony of Peace."

"I can hear '*Yankee Doodle*' and '*Dixie*' all through it, though," said Rollo.

"Yes," said Santa Claus, giving the boy a tight squeeze, "I'm glad you noticed that, for those are the two songs that above all others tell the beautiful story of the Brotherhood of Man, the story of Peace and Good-will which is the sweetest story that ever was told. When I found that the strains of '*Dixie*' and '*Yankee Doodle*' could be united into a beautiful hymn of

America, it seemed to me that we might take all the others, too, and work up an Anthem which at Christmas-tide should carry the message of Peace all over the world. This is the result."

"It is very good," said Rollo. "But why do you have it sung by Jack-in-the-Boxes?"

"Well," said Santa Claus, with a laugh, "I wanted to try it at its worst to start with. It seemed to me that if it sounded fine and clear and true with a lot of Jack-in-the-Box voices, I need have no fear for it when it came to be sung by boys and girls the world over."

Rollo leaned back in Santa Claus' lap and listened to the song as the Jacks sang it over and over again. Whether it was the song or the warmth of the room, or the softness of dear old Santa Claus' embrace or not, I don't know, but the lad grew drowsy, and his little head drooped on the good Saint's fur-covered waistcoat. The song was still ringing in his ears as just for a teeny weeny bit of a second he dropped off—

       *   *   *   *

          *   *   *

       *   *   *   *

CHAPTER XI

Home Again

And then—where was he? Surely this was not Santa Claus' lap on which he sat, but the bank of a sea—and—who was that imperious figure sitting up there on the rock—not Santa Claus, nor Father Time—but—

"Father Neptune, at your service, Rollo," said the handsome old creature, waving his trident over the waters. "You have spent all the extra hours Father Time gave you, my lad, and I am now stilling the sea so that you may sail safely home again."

"B–but where is Santa Claus?" asked Rollo.

"Packing the toys," replied Father Neptune. "Christmas will soon be here, and he is making ready. He brought you to me while you were sleeping, and I promised to see you safe home again, because, as he said, you are a boy worth having. Why, he told me you would be a 9—4—27—3—10 some day."

"Oh, dear!" cried Rollo. "I wish I knew what those figures meant."

"You will—as soon as it is good for you, my son," replied Father Neptune, "in about forty-seven years, I should say."

*   *   *   *
  *   *   *
*   *   *   *

"Look out for that buoy ahead there!" cried a fierce voice. Rollo rubbed his eyes sleepily again, and lo! another change had come upon him. He was not on land but in a great flat-bottomed boat, speeding out to sea, and in the stern stood no less a personage than the great Wooden Indian that Rollo had often admired in front of a cigar-store not far from his home. He was a terrible-looking old fellow, but Rollo had known him for so long a time that if he ever had had any fear of him, it had long ago worn off.

"Hello, Lo," said he, drowsily, as he recognized his companion. "Where am I now?"

"Going home," replied the Indian, fiercely. "Where you ought to be. Do you know what time it is?"

"Haven't the slightest idea," he replied. "What time is it?"

*   *   *   *
   *   *   *
*   *   *   *

The sea and the boat and the Wooden Indian all faded from view as the lad spoke, and Rollo suddenly became conscious of the glow of a crackling log-fire in front of him, and the soft embrace of a huge armchair about him, and looking up sleepily, he caught sight of a pair of eyes that were gazing down affectionately into his. He repeated his question.

"What time is it?"

"Supper-time, Sleepy-head," was the response, and Rollo found himself suddenly caught up in a pair of arms that he loved. "You must have met the Sandman pretty early to-day," said the owner of the arms.

"Why, yes, Papa, I did," Rollo answered.

"But—"

"He filled your eyes up pretty full, did he?"

"Why, no," said Rollo. "I haven't been asleep. I've been— I've been Embleming."

"What?" cried his Daddy, to whom the word was new.

"Embleming," he answered, and then he told his father all about Emblemland, and the strange, kindly folk who lived there, and his father said it was a most extraordinary story, in which Rollo and I both agreed so fully that, from his notes sent to me two or three days later, I decided to put it down upon paper and send it to you.

It isn't very much of a story, of course, and Rollo and I make no particular claim for it except that it gave him pleasure to live it, and me some delight to write it, because it was fun for him while it lasted and it enabled me to renew my own acquaintance with at least two dear friends of my youth, Santa Claus and the Sandman. I love the first for the fine spirit of good-will, to the keeping alive of which he devotes his life, and as for the Sandman, I have ever loved to be with

> *... the fellow strange and odd*
> *Who guides you through the land of Nod;*
> *Who takes you to the Vale of Dreams,*
> *Where nothing's quite the thing it seems*
> *And empty plans seem wondrous schemes;*

and between you and me and the lamp-post, I am inclined to believe with Rollo's father that the Sandman was at the bottom of the whole thing, after all, and that if it hadn't been for his invisible presence at the very beginning with the Dolphin and the Boat, we should never have heard of *Rollo in Emblemland* at all.

Eachtraí Eilíse i dTír na nIontas
Alice in Irish, 2007

Lastall den Scáthán agus a bhFuair Eilís Ann Roimpi
Looking-Glass in Irish, 2009

Alys in Pow an Anethow
Alice in Cornish, 2009

La Aventuroj de Alicio en Mirlando
Alice in Esperanto, 2009

Les Aventures d'Alice au pays des merveilles
Alice in French, 2010

Alice's Abenteuer im Wunderland
Alice in German, 2010

Le Avventure di Alice nel Paese delle Meraviglie
Alice in Italian, 2010

Alicia in Terra Mirabili
Alice in Latin, 2010

Contoyrtyssyn Ealish ayns Çheer ny Yindyssyn
Alice in Manx, 2010

Alice's Äventyr i Sagolandet
Alice in Swedish, 2010

Anturiaethau Alys yng Ngwlad Hud
Alice in Welsh, 2010

Lightning Source UK Ltd.
Milton Keynes UK
02 September 2010

159308UK00001B/3/P